I am Mary

Esther E. Hawkins

2014
Merry Christmas
Aunt Barbie!
love you, Janon

Cover artwork © 2013 by Christina Steele
Hebrew translation: *The Lord has taken away my shame.*

Cover design by Melissa Vanderlinden with Delve Photography • www.delvephotography.com

Yet you brought me out of the womb;
you made me trust in you even at my mother's breast.
From birth I was cast upon you;
from my mother's womb you have been my God.
Psalm 22: 9-10 (NIV)

Table of Contents

Introduction

Simple, sweet, innocent, demure; I had always pictured Mary as many of us have, according to the pictorial representations that display her delicate beauty bathed in an celestial glow. She tenderly caresses a chubby, smiling babe and draws the audience into a sense of peace and tranquility that could only accompany the mother of the Son of God.

At some point, I began to doubt; was it my own experiences that caused me to challenge what I had always presumed? My question was simply this, "What kind of woman do you have to be to be chosen as the mother of Christ?" I was curious, and as Mary's story began to unfold, I realized that it was not as serene as we would perhaps have hoped. I wondered; how much of her story can women and mothers relate to today?

We see Mary's struggle during the annunciation when she is greeted by an angel who affirms her as God's *"highly favored!"* (Luke 1:28 New International Version)

Her response exposes an understandable measure of insecurity when she is described as being *"troubled at his words and wondered what kind of greeting this might be."* (Luke 1:29)

The angel immediately goes on to say, *"Do not be afraid, Mary."* (Luke 1:30)

Fear would be an appropriate response under the circumstances, but is it appropriate for Mary? Certainly many of us could relate, but would God really choose a woman whose first reaction to seeing an angel was fear?

The angel goes on to explain what is about to take place, *"You will conceive and give birth to a son, and you are to call him Jesus. He will be great and will be called the Son of the Most High. The Lord God will give him the throne of his father David, and he will reign over Jacob's descendants forever; his kingdom will never end."* (Luke 1:31-33)

Mary, along with the whole Jewish nation, had been anticipating and longing for the coming of the Messiah. Much celebration would be expected upon his arrival, as it would mark freedom from the cruelty that had surrounded their people for generations. To have been chosen for such a historic and monumental task would be an honor beyond comprehension. Should she fall on her face in awe and wonder? Should she kneel in unwavering acceptance? The Messiah's appearing had been prophesied in the Old Testament, *"Therefore the Lord himself will give you a sign: The virgin will conceive and give birth to a son, and will call him Immanuel."* (Isaiah 7:14) The angel's words would not have been completely unfamiliar, and yet Mary's response again betrays her when she asks, *"How can this be since I am a virgin?"* (Luke 1:34)

We can assume that Mary has a heart after God; a loving relationship with Him in which He sees in her a heart that is humble, trustworthy and deeply devoted to Him. Yet, her instinct is to doubt.

As I explored this Mary, she began to sound much more real and like many women that I know; scared, insecure and full of doubts. God had already chosen Mary despite her weakness. We see the story unfold beautifully as she is gently invited into acceptance of this invitation.

In Luke 1:36, the angel shares a story, *"And behold, even your relative Elizabeth has also conceived a son in her old age: and she who was called barren is now in her sixth month. For nothing will be impossible with God."*

There is a moment here when Mary is confronted with the impossible being made possible. There is perhaps the feeling that she would not be alone. This simple testimony breathes life into her heart and her response is finally one of strength, and acceptance.

"Behold the bond slave of the Lord: may it be done to me according to your word." (Luke 1:38)

In this book, I hope to explore Mary's experiences in the light of her choice, but also knowing that she was a woman plagued with the same struggles that many of us face daily. What has become apparent is that God took a huge risk entrusting the life of His Son into the hands of two people who were unremarkable, poor and inadequate. Mary and Joseph not only had to face their own fears, but had to negotiate a culture steeped in religion and rules, and a time period in history that is set apart for its brutality.

The gospels reveal to us that Jesus lived a life of betrayal, rejection, violence, humiliation, pain and ultimate death.

I Am Mary

The story that I have sought to tell gives us a brief insight into the battle that was waged simply to bring Jesus to birth. How profoundly His life has impacted millions through the ages, a life marked not from birth but from conception.

iv

One

I woke up slowly as the scorch of spring sun fell over my face. It must have been midmorning as the windows were small and high in the wall, framing the sun long after dawn. My dreams dissipated and made way for reality to settle in heavily. Eyes squeezed; my breaths became shallower and my throat burned with thirst. I smelled the remains of breakfast drying out in the pot and my stomach wretched. I groaned as I pulled the blanket over my head, hoping that sleep might draw me away again.

The door opened and closed as my mother returned from the well. She set the pitcher down and stirred the pot, muttering something under her breath. She smoothed her tunic and turned this way and that as she always did, as though she wasn't sure what she should do next. Her feet padded softly towards me and she sat next to me on the mattress.

"You're still sleeping?" she asked tenderly. "Are you sick? It has been several days that you have been late to go to the fields."

"I'm fine *Ima*," I responded lethargically. "Perhaps it is time for me to go to the *mikvah*. I always feel tired at this time of the month."

"Perhaps," she answered, concern etched in her voice.

I knew that I could not work in the fields that day. I decided to go to the mikvah, even though it was not my time. I hoped that the women did not keep track of each other's cycles, as they would surely realize that it had been many weeks since I had last attended. I rolled onto hands and knees and rose slowly to keep my head from spinning. Supported against the wall, I made my way across the room, keeping my head low so that I would not pass out. Sweat beaded on my forehead and I was anything but graceful as I lurched to the pillow and sat waiting for Ima to give me something to drink. I took small sips of water, only enough to hydrate my mouth but not enough to reach my stomach. I felt sure that anything I swallowed would not stay down for long.

"Eating may help," Ima coaxed.

I was already thin and a missed meal made me look gaunt. I forced myself to eat, thankful that each mouthful made me feel a little better. I revived slowly and washed my face and hands in the barrel of rainwater that stood in the corner. Ima circled me with her chores. She said nothing else but her silence bored into my skin. I shuddered and gathered my basket of rags and clean clothes before hurrying outside. I knew every alley and backstreet and made my way cautiously so that I could avoid contact, hoping that no one would stop me. I found the mikvah nestled into a hill on the east side of the village. Trees leaned over the building protectively, branches beckoning me into their haven. I entered through the low doorway and let the cool air drench over me, laying my belongings on the bench and adjusting to the dim light. I was relieved to find the room empty except for an older woman who was asleep on the other side of the room. I sat cross-legged on the floor and leaned my head back against the bench. My focus rested on the gentle swish of water in the pool.

The mikvah was separated from village life, as women were considered unclean during menstruation until they were cleansed. Normally I enjoyed the ritual, especially as it meant a return to normal life after being isolated for seven days. For a young girl this time of separation seemed to stretch on endlessly. Often, the girls would gather at the mikvah and each month it was a reunion of souls.

Today, I welcomed the solitude. I was afraid to look into another's eyes, afraid that they would search my soul and expose me. I drew in a deep breath as my stomach heaved again and I struggled upwards, staggering out of the mikvah to throw up my breakfast in the trees that bordered the hillside. I made my way slowly back inside, weak and exhausted despite many hours of sleep. The commotion had woken the other woman who I barely recognized. We allowed travelers to purify themselves too. She was large and smelled bad despite having bathed already. I greeted her formally and she came close.

"You are Joachim's daughter?" she asked rhetorically.

I nodded, puzzled as to how she knew me and why it would matter.

"A kind man. He has helped my family many times. He helps many. I hope you are not a disappointment to such a kind man." She narrowed her eyes and then left, patting me on the shoulder as she disappeared through the door.

"Oh God," I whispered. "Oh God, what have I done?"

I let the stillness wrap around and stretched out a mat on the cool tile floor. I lay, panting breaths, head hung listlessly. A gecko scuttled over the broken tile and up the wall, stopping briefly to swallow a fly before squeezing through a hole to the roof. I longed for life to return to such simplicity. How was it possible that everything could become so unbearably complex so quickly? Just one simple mistake was all it took, just one moment of confusion. I sobbed involuntarily. I didn't know what I was going to do. I had cried out to God for help but felt nothing. I had always felt so close to him. For as long as I could remember, I had loved him. Even as a child, I had fasted, praying as I played. I sang to Him while I worked. I listened as the men recited the Torah so that I could memorize portions of scripture. I could enter effortlessly into His presence, losing myself in the wonder of who He was; overwhelmed by His goodness. So why, when I needed Him the most, did He feel absent, cold, unavailable? I tried to draw strength from what I had experienced in the past and yet I felt so physically drained, so weak and so very alone, that strength only seemed to ebb.

Voices passed by on the road below and stirred me back to my senses. I sat up quickly to prepare for immersion. I brushed my long hair and then undressed. The water was crisp and perfectly clear. I sank slowly into the small pool and let the water cover me. I stayed under for as long as I could and reluctantly came up, gasping for air. How easily this could all be over. I brushed the thought away and hurried out of the pool to dress. The water had refreshed and I felt my heart beating violently as it forced blood through my veins. I was invigorated and my stomach growled, this time with hunger. I picked a few figs on my way home, their sweetness gentle on my belly. I looked closely at the houses, the orchards and gardens. Sights that I had taken for granted my whole life now felt unfamiliar and awkward. A wave from a neighbor unnerved me. Places that I had previously longed to run to, I now avoided.

One of my earliest memories was roaming these streets and hills on my father's shoulders. He was a slight man with a limp and yet to me he was strong and able. I would run my chubby fingers through his curly hair and cling to him as he made his way through the village.

"Not so tight my daughter," he would laugh.

I would giggle and rest my chin on the top of his head, waiting for him to tell me a story or to point out a flower or bug.

"Look, *Abba!* An eagle," I called.

"No, just a sparrow," he replied. "But no less significant."

"Shalom, neighbor!" he called to a passerby. "How is life today? Is there any way I can assist you?"

My abba was known for his big heart and unceasing willingness to help anyone in need. Ima was often exasperated by him as she worked tirelessly at home while he was helping someone else. He always anticipated her frustration and would walk in the house with a handful of wildflowers and a pomegranate, singing to her while he whisked her around the room in a dance.

"My love," he whispered tenderly. "I am inspired to

serve because of the way that you serve me."

Each time she would end up laughing as he kissed her and then complimented her on her housekeeping.

"My Anah, how clean the floors are today. You would think that they were laid with tile, not dirt, and how tasty is the bread. I think it is the best loaf I've ever eaten."

"Oh you scoundrel!" she would jibe, it is the same loaf I have made every day of our marriage."

I sat curled up on a pillow watching as their love filled the room. I delighted in them and longed to be drawn into their embrace. Abba, so strong and kind; Ima so sure and capable. I often felt very small in the room.

I made it home from the mikvah with no encounters on the path. I climbed the narrow stone steps on the outside of the house to the roof where I washed my clothes and lay them out to dry. The sun was on its long descent to dusk and I saw the villagers in the fields below gathering their crops and herding the animals. Somehow I would have to return to the fields tomorrow. I sighed. I did not know how I would manage to work all day, or how I could pretend to all of my friends that nothing was wrong. I had never had a secret before. Innocent fantasies and childish observations had always been shared avidly and whispered among friends with giggles and cries of delight. No secret had ever been so weighty or so devastating that it had to be held close and shared with no one.

"Come, child, it is time for dinner," Ima called as Abba came around the corner.

He stopped at the bottom of the stairs as I made my way down, taking his outstretched hand as I reached the last few steps. He took my face in his hands. I bit my lip and looked over his shoulder, unable to look him in the eye. I could see the concern in his face; I could feel the agony of the disconnect between us.

"My child, Abba loves you. I am pleased with you," his voice was steady but his soul wept.

"I know, Abba," I croaked, throat tightening.

"I have failed you," he spoke with pain. "You know in your head and yet you do not know in your heart."

He wrapped his arms around me and I buried my face in his shoulder, arms hanging limply by my side.

"Will you still love me when you know what shame I have brought upon us?" I asked silently, unable to voice my thoughts.

Abba went into the house and I leaned against climbing vines and flowers that scaled the wall. Their fragrance soothed.

"God, Abba God, are you pleased with me?" My heart cried out to know.

Do not be afraid. [1]

Those words echoed through my mind. They were the only words of instruction that I had been given and yet they seemed trite when the weight of fear threatened to crush. I clung to them, to the memory of them spoken, and hope pressed my aching soul.

Two

I pulled away from the vines and dragged my feet into the house. Ima sat across the room, face in hands, Abba's arm wrapped around her shoulder. They both looked up sharply as I entered. Ima's face white and Abba's sadness more visible.

I froze. Should I confess or would I give away more than they already knew? They would have to know soon enough but I wasn't ready yet to tell them.

"Come, Mary," Abba motioned for me to sit. The smell of fresh bread and olives taunted my delicate stomach. I ran anxiety-drenched hands down my tunic, ears filled with my beating heart.

Abba took my hand in his as Ima placed hers on my knee.

"Mary, I have some news for you that will be hard to hear. I have yet to pursue the details but I wanted you to hear this first from us." He paused and lifted my chin so that we made eye contact. "Joseph has left the village, Mary. No one knows why or where he has gone."

I sighed with relief. At least I had a little more time.

"Please, Mary, do not be disheartened. I believe that we will find him and be able to determine what has taken place. Joseph is already a son to me; he will listen to the voice of a father."

"Mary," Ima joined in.

I had not responded and painful silence was difficult to endure.

"Mary," she repeated softly. "There is the possibility that this means that Joseph no longer intends to marry you. I know this is devastating news and we are heartbroken too."

She broke down and buried her face in her hands again. I showed no emotion even though I felt the swirl of tides crashing inside.

"God is in control," I muttered blandly.

"Yes, Mary," Abba echoed. "God is in control."

I turned to dinner, still hot on the fire, and served my parents. I ate out of necessity but made my way to bed as quickly as possible. I already knew that Joseph was long gone.

I had waited to tell him until I knew for sure that it was real and not just a dream. Upon the first signs, I had made my way excitedly to his workshop to share the news. My only trepidation was in how I should word such an announcement, not in how he would respond. He was my beloved, my protector. It never occurred to me that really he was just a man.

I knocked boldly on his door.

"Is someone there?" The hammering stopped. "Who is there?" he asked again.

"It is Mary," I answered cheerfully.

The door opened. Joseph, tall and rugged filled the doorway as he wiped labored hands on cloth tucked into his belt. He looked up and down the street.

"What are you doing here, Mary?" he asked, the kindness of his tone tinged with awkwardness. "Why did your father not accompany you? You should not come to see me alone."

"I know, Joseph," I responded humbly. "I need to speak with you privately. Can we walk somewhere together where we can be seen but not overheard?"

My sudden request was a pressure on him. He was a steady, careful man who worked methodically and with great care and integrity. I realized my mistake and tried to compensate.

"I'm sorry, Joseph. I will leave and wait for you to send for me. Please though, we must speak soon."

I turned to leave, embarrassed by my lack of discretion but Joseph stopped me.

"No, Mary. We must talk now if your heart is heavy. My work can wait. Just let me wash my face and hands. I will meet you by the Fig."

I nodded, my spirit revived, and hurried along the street to the edge of town. The hill rolled out beneath me and I followed the meandering trail to the cluster of fig trees. The Fig was a common meeting place as it had grown large and its branches sprawled sideways providing seating that overlooked the valley. The path was well traveled and I was confident that our meeting there would not look suspicious. Joseph met me moments later and sat on the opposite branch. I wasn't sure how to begin but he opened up our conversation.

"How are the wedding plans, Mary? I believe it might be sooner than we expect. I am getting plenty of work and am making good progress on our home."

He looked so handsome, so full of anticipation. I appreciated his reassurance of our imminent life together.

"I am happy, Joseph. You are an excellent craftsman and I know that our home will be beautiful and filled with …." Words trailed off as my thoughts pressed for attention.

"I must talk with you, Joseph. Something wonderful and yet terrible has occurred."

I waited so that I could watch his reaction. A small readjustment in his position was the only indication of his discomfort.

"Go head, Mary, I'm listening," he encouraged.

"The Messiah, the one we have been waiting for. He is coming."

Joseph's eyes narrowed ever so slightly. I hadn't yet told him anything he didn't already know.

"I was visited by a messenger, an angel. He told me that I had been chosen to bare the child who would come to save us. I was unsure if it was really true but it has been several weeks and now I know that I am carrying a child."

Joseph pulled back slightly and pressed his hands into the branch on either side of his legs. He paused and then stood slowly, pausing again. He walked several steps away from the tree, looking over the valley.

"You are pregnant," he whispered somberly.

"Yes," I replied unapologetically. "I am carrying the Messiah."

A chill entered my heart as I realized that the conversation was not going how I had expected. There had been no thought, no consideration that Joseph would be anything but filled with joy and amazement as I had been. The privilege of this role and the thought of being chosen to fulfill it was immense, and yet I realized that I had been naïve in my assessment of it.

Joseph was silent for a long time and I dared not speak again.

"Why have you waited until how to tell me?" he asked.

"I wanted to be sure." My voice already betrayed feelings of dejection. "I didn't know when it would happen. I hoped that it would happen after our wedding."

"After the wedding…" Joseph muttered, turning back and making his way closer.

"You are telling me that the God of Israel has chosen you to be the mother of the Messiah?"

He turned, indicating that his question did not require a response.

My hands began to shake and my mind went blank. I didn't know what to think.

Why had God chosen me? Had he made a mistake?

"I am nothing," I whispered to myself.

Had I made it all up? Had it been a dream? But then, what of the pregnancy? Perhaps I was just sick. Perhaps I had been violated and had spun a story to cover myself. Perhaps this was all a lie….

Tears welled and I could not bear to look at Joseph. I slid off the branch and stumbled back up the trail to the street where I ran home without pausing for breath.

I had not dared to speak of it since, instead just trying to make sense of it all. My mind was filled with confusion but the memory of the angel was still so clear. My mind swirled with accusation and doubt. I was plagued by my inadequacy and found great shame in my naivety. I did not see Joseph again and worried every day about who he had told and what he would do. I continued to work in the field but I was soon overcome with nausea and exhaustion. For seven days I pretended to be menstruating so I could stay at home in seclusion. I hoped that something would change after that but the unraveling of my story had begun. Now that Joseph had left town, questions would be rampant and I would be at the center of speculation or pity, neither of which I wanted.

Ima woke me early the next morning.

"How are you today?" she asked placing a hand on my back. "Perhaps you should stay home, people are starting to talk about Joseph's disappearance."

I shrugged and rose so that I could get ready to leave with the other girls as they passed by. We had worked together in the fields for many seasons and our labor made us strong and healthy. The hot beat of sun overhead and the cool, earthy smell of the dirt below were where my soul found respite. The laughter of my friends made our days easy with love and camaraderie. There was always a bustle of energy as each season brought with it a fresh wave of anticipation; planting, tending, harvesting. The rhythm moved us gently through life. The men in the fields and the shepherds on the hills protected us and led us with strength and humility. Their wisdom and knowledge of the earth left little room for surprises. It was rare in the Galilee region to have a poor harvest. Our men worked tirelessly to tend the harvest and livestock, and were a formidable opponent against pestilence, bugs or weather. Our people survived on what they knew and what had been passed down. Year after year we lived, ate and survived on the predictability of our lifestyle and culture.

If the girls had heard rumors, they would probably pass by without knocking on my door and then I would stay home. I heard their songs as they approached and waited, hands clasped. The usual knock encouraged me and I slipped out of the door to join the back of their group. Each one smiled and greeted me as they always had. Sari tucked her arm through mine and kissed my cheek.

"We have missed you," she said without suspicion. "You must come for dinner tonight. Ima has made your favorite cake and we have much to talk about."

I froze but she pulled me along with the sweetness of her voice as she joined in the song. I did my best to pretend that everything was the same but when I opened my mouth to sing, I found that I was unable to make a sound. We paired up to work but I longed for quietness over the joviality of the group.

We stopped for lunch earlier than usual and sat together under the trees to cool off and eat. Sari stroked my hair and I leaned my head on her lap as I often did. I closed my eyes, trying to stay awake as the girls chatted around me. I felt detached, unable to identify with their senseless conversation and knowing that I may never feel like one of them again. A lull suddenly settled and then hushed voices swept through the group. I opened my eyes as the laborers dissipated back to the fields. Was I imagining it or were they looking at me as they left? I sat upright and prepared to join my friends. Standing slowly, I stretched, reaching out to Sari to steady myself. She pulled her arm away and looked at me with disappointment. My gaze fell on the rest of the girls, as one by one each tried to hide their shock and disdain.

"Is it true?" hissed Sari. "Is it true, Mary?"

I felt my face burn with shame.

"I…. I….. what…?" I stammered.

"I can't believe it," she exclaimed. "What have you done?"

We spent the rest of the day in stunned silence. I worked alone and watched the rest of the group gravitate to each other.

I felt sick and desperately alone.

Three

The air was thick with humidity. I had to walk slowly to catch each breath and wipe the sweat off my forehead. The way home looked steeper and more arduous than ever as a steaming haze rose off each rock that scattered the narrow road. I had walked this trail countless times before. Life was a simple sequence of routines that I fulfilled without question. My role in the family, my role in life was secure and so my daily walk down the hill to work in the fields was as much a part of me as my own skin. Each of us was embedded in what our lives provided functionally for our families and community. The sense of tradition among us was strong. It pervaded our thoughts, our language and dictated the structure of our weeks. It should have been an uncomplicated life.

The screeching of a buzzard overhead interrupted my thoughts and I shuddered under its influence. My face burned and I draped my head and shoulders for shelter. My basket of wheat slipped from my hands giving me a chance to catch my breath. I turned, as I always did, to survey the beauty. The Galilee region soaked in the sun and, in return, bestowed abundance upon the land. I had heard of places even more beautiful, that overflowed with the richness of the green earth. Lands with trees that soared into the sky creating a canopy of coolness to the soft earth below where streams and rivers meandered; where wildlife strolled and fruit as big as the sun hung from their limbs, and flowers dripped with sweet nectar. I had heard that there used to be such places in my own country; places of unparalleled beauty but I had not seen them myself. These were stories passed down through the generations. Stories we retold with such precision that we could recite them together; stories that we believed so strongly that they became part of the fiber of our being.

I looked out over the orchards and fields that laced the hillside and valley below in a rich tapestry of colors and textures. I wondered how something I had seen so often could still fill me with such pleasure. Rough roads offered travelers and carts little respite. Shepherds had created trails through simple repetition, and huge oaks spread their branches over sleeping farmers who spent many hours on the hills with the animals. The gnarly looking olive trees promised a bounty of fruit, and the wild looking fig trees tempted us daily as we anticipated their yield. Spring had been gracious to us and crops were bursting. The men were still toiling after a long day gathering wheat and finishing last month's barley harvest.

The girls who I had worked with in the fields had gone on ahead. Tears pricked my eyes. We had always taken the road home together and lightened the work of the day with stories and laughter. They were ten steps ahead of me but the distance increased until I was finally alone. The ground shimmered in the last rays of sun. The hill that, just minutes before had stretched out ahead, now descended into the valley.

I turned towards my village that rose up out of the hillside. Our homes blended into rocky outcroppings; unassuming structures that shielded their occupants from the blazing sun of summer. I could name each home, each inhabitant. The sound of children laughing and playing filled every street, a sweet melody. I was barely more than a child myself but adulthood came upon us quickly. Poverty forced our hand and we were trained from a young age to work. It was the way of life for us. It was all I had known and all that I could ever expect. I tried to be thankful, and yet there always lurked a darkness that I could not explain, a shifting shadow that followed but never took form. I sighed deeply under the weight of sadness that I had carried silently and inexplicably for as long as I could remember.

The buzzard screeched again and seemed closer. I picked up my basket and hurried up the hill to home where Ima would be waiting for the supplies to start dinner. I reached the outskirts of the village and ran my hand along the side of the first house. Lines had been scoured along the mud wall by the swords of soldiers who had passed through recently. Manure from their horses still littered the road. The Roman occupation hadn't affected the routine of daily life, but it had struck a blow to our hearts. They were unparalleled in their brutality and held little, if any, regard for us. They were larger than life. These men were not like the simple farming folk of my people; skin scorched from long days in the sun, and hands rough and calloused. The centurions were pale; faces scarred from battle. Their eyes betrayed the coldness that only comes from seeing lives expire before you. There was an unspoken understanding among us that we were nothing in their eyes, less than dogs and we were to bow to their demands or face the certain consequences. Nazareth, barely a scratch on the map of Israel, was protected by our insignificance, most of the action taking place in or closer to Jerusalem, which was several days journey away. However, our position close to the road in the valley meant that we often witnessed the march of armies from the north. The ground shook with footsteps, and rumbled under the enormity of their chariots, hundreds at times. We rarely elicited more than a glance.

I turned the corner into the coolness of the alley between two houses. Steps rose up at the far end of the pathway; I was almost home. As I walked towards the stairs, heavy, raspy breaths approached quickly behind me. I turned to see who was there when I was grabbed harshly and pushed up against the wall. At first I couldn't see. I frantically grabbed at my scarf, pushing it away from my face to catch sight of who had pinned me. I looked up into the face of towering evil that blocked the light. I could taste the darkness. My arm throbbed with pain as he continued to hold me tight. Leaning forward, he moved his other hand and pressed it against the wall above my head. The hard metal of his armor oppressed; cords draped gaudy and arrogant. Rancid breath reeked of alcohol and spit dripped from cracked lips; eyes, narrow, bloodshot and rife with wickedness. I shook with panic but couldn't cry out. Instinct forced me just to breathe, to survive. I knew that I would not be rescued. No man I knew was capable or equipped to stand up to such a beast. At best, any kind of intervention that could free me would be a death sentence for my rescuer. I had heard many times of the horrors of Roman justice. The innocence of the children in our village was largely sheltered but as the adults talked and the children played, our ears were tuned to listen. There was no reasoning behind their death sentences, just pure hatred towards our people. Eyes were gouged, hands and feet severed, many were crucified for the price of a stolen loaf of bread. Torture was their sport. Humiliation and power was their game and we, the humble, were their target. The weakest and most vulnerable of us were exposed to their shocking violence.

I remember when I was barely a toddler, watching a cat in the barn. I hid, fascinated by this creature that normally mewed and curled itself upon our laps. Its softness and cuteness drew endless enjoyment for the children, but here that same cat turned into a predator. I saw it transform in an instant from a big-eyed, furry friend into a sleek, narrow-eyed killer. Its back sunk low as it crawled silently and patiently towards its prey, never a sound; pure focus. Then in an instant it pounced and sprang several feet to its target that I had been unable to see; a tiny mouse. My little lips quivered, but I was frozen to the spot. The cat was not content to simply kill and eat its victim. I noticed that its paw had simply trapped the mouse's tail. The sound emitted was tragic as the cat played and tormented it until the final moment of inevitable death.

The evening sun that had always cheered me after a long

day in the fields seemed to slide sadly and helplessly towards the horizon. Its power that caused the earth to burst forth, and drew us all out of our homes each day, was worthless to me now. Light was overpowered by darkness as walls masked the glowing orb and cast a shadow over me. I shivered as warmth retreated, and then shook as coldness entered my soul. The only heat now was from his breath that stung my neck and caused my eyes to glisten with tears. There would be no escape; the price of my life would be no sacrifice for this man. His recounting of my death would likely be entertainment among his peers and superiors. He leaned in closer and I turned my face to escape his eye and toxicity. His breathing turned shallower and his lips began to snarl like an animal.

"I've heard about you," he hissed in my ear.

I gasped. How could he know? I had never seen this man before. My mind raced, clamoring. Darkness continued to intensify, causing depths of shadow to dance and taunt. My senses sharpened to the sounds of dusk. The pounding of blood in my head competed with the repulsive smell of the beast that cascaded in waves.

I clutched my hands to my belly.

"That's right, you know exactly what I'm talking about. You can't keep secrets around here you filthy whore."

Four

Tears slid as he took a shaky, dirty finger and scraped it down the side of my face and onto my breast. My head spun. As he drew closer, overpowering, a gust of wind coursed through the alleyway knocking us both off balance. This was not unusual due to our position on the hillside, but that day had been particularly calm. Bewilderment crossed his face as he stumbled to regain his footing. It was all I needed. His grip on my arm slackened; I slipped from his grasp and fled. Disappearing up the steps at the end of the alley, I didn't look back, my window of escape potentially closing in an instant. I clambered up the stairs and erupted onto the roof with great gasps. The setting sun cast its soft pink glow over my face and warmed me. It had not abandoned me after all. I half ran, half stumbled through the maze of narrow streets, scrambling across flat roofs and leaping between houses to lose my attacker. I reached home and crashed through the wooden doorway, leaving it swinging wildly behind. Ima sat on the dirt floor grinding barley into flour for our evening meal. I stood in the middle of the small, sparse room, hair streaked with sweat and clinging to my panic stricken face; lungs burning as I drew in desperate breaths.

"What is it?" Ima cried as she leaped from the floor and grabbed my shoulders before I collapsed.

I couldn't speak but my face drained color. She put her face closer to mine, studying my eyes.

"What did you do?" she whispered.

My body stiffened and we held our breath as the sounds of chaos from the streets reached our ears. My assailant was pursuing me, blindly crashing through dusty lanes and banging on every door he found. Women screamed and children clutched by arms, wailed.

"Where are you?" he slurred.

I pictured his drunken, drooling lips; evil imprinted on my eyes tight shut.

"You'll be sorry you were ever born when I get my hands on you…." His voice trailed. He was getting closer.

Ima closed and bolted the door and led me quickly to the back of the house where reed mattresses were piled high in the corner

"We'll hide in the grotto. Be as quiet as you can," she instructed.

I threw my basket by the cooking pot and helped her move the mats, legs shaking. We uncovered a small hole in the ground, just large enough for a man to pass through to a secret room below.

"Hurry," Ima urged. "We must be silent."

I dropped down through the hole to a small staircase that led to a room only big enough to hold six men. Darkness closed in as Ima covered the hole and I made my way blindly along the cool, stone walls. I sat, back pressed into the corner and wrapped myself in shaking arms. Ima followed and held me as we crouched petrified against the wall. I let out a silent cry and held my breath as pounding unleashed on the door upstairs.

"Where is she?" the soldier slurred.

By now, an eerie stillness had settled over our tiny hamlet. This event would be devastating. The door crashed open and Goliath pounded the earth above. Table tossed and stools splintered. The moment lasted forever but suddenly the door slammed. We dared not move in case he came back. The secrecy of the grotto lulled me and I jumped when Ima finally released her grip.

"Mary," she spoke gently now as her slender, icy fingers searched for my face and brushed the hair from my eyes. "Mary, what is happening? You have been quiet for so many weeks and now this? Please tell me."

Her tone soothed and I knew that I could not keep my secret much longer. Perhaps she already knew. I recalled the looks and comments from my friends and the curses from a stranger... how could he possibly know? My mouth filled with vile liquid and my head became light. I managed not to vomit.

"Mary." She was sterner now. "I know something is wrong, you must tell me."

I was thankful for the darkness. Something wrong. Something was terribly, terribly wrong.

My throat burned; voice just a whisper, "I'm pregnant."

Body stiffened; breath drawn in. I searched for her eyes, for understanding, for love but I saw nothing; black emptiness.

I closed my own eyes, wishing that the hole I had climbed into would cave in above my head.

"So it's true," she whispered, voice tinged with amazement, words barely audible.

She turned to me although I could only see the outline of her face, and took my shaking hand in hers. It was several minutes before she spoke again.   " T h e r e have been rumors," she said. "It has been two moon cycles since you have been to the mikvah and only five since your betrothal. I saw you go yesterday but your rags were not soiled."

"It's not what you think, Ima." I spoke desperately.

"Hush child," she said. "We will wait for Abba."

I dreaded the thought of telling him. My father had always been my confidante but how could I tell him such news with no guarantee that he would believe me? Lamplight finally streamed through the opening as Abba motioned for us to come out. My body stiff and sore, I crawled across the floor and made my way up into the house, squinting. The cool night air refreshed but mingled with dinner ruined. Ima took my arm and led me to a mat so I could lie down and warm up. The smell of burnt bread filled the house as Abba removed the blackened loaf from the stove.

"Stay and rest," Ima said. "I'll get you water."

I watched as she dipped a chalk pot deep into the water and set it on the floor to filter. Abba and Ima moved silently around each other, a glance here, a muttered whisper there. I wished that I could crawl back into the grotto.

"I'm sorry, Ima," I whispered, parched lips trembling.

"Here, eat this," she said gently as she handed me a plate of sun-dried figs. "You must keep up your strength."

I dozed until Abba sat beside me and put his hand on my shoulder. He helped me up and pushed tea brewed with hyssop into my hand. I sipped while he and Ima pulled the brightly colored cushions from the corner of the room. I noticed that the table had been reset and we sat around it to eat, its stout legs now supporting vegetable barley soup and a freshly baked loaf.

"I'm sorry I was not here, Anah," he said as they sat down together.

"Has he gone?" Ima asked, her voice still betraying the emotion she had felt hours before.

"Yes, he was seen leaving to join the other soldiers on their way to Tiberias. We don't know why he was here alone."

They paused and silence hung heavily in the air.

Ima sat and ate quietly, head bowed. I could not eat. I grasped for hope.

Finally Abba spoke, "Mary, Ima has told me the news."

My eyes fell to the floor and I dared not look at him, afraid that seeing the pain would cause my heart to break.

"It's not what you think, Abba." I repeated the appeal that I had made to Ima.

Abba sighed and set his bowl back on the table.

"Then what must I think, Mary?" He tried to remain calm but I sensed the agitation in his voice. "Nazareth is rife with speculation. People are asking if you have had relations with this soldier before. Others are accusing Joseph but no one has seen him for weeks. Answers are being sought and I can only help you if I know the truth. Mary, you must realize the gravity of your situation."

I reeled.

"Mary!" Abba had never shouted at me before. He clasped my face in his hand; cheeks pressed in, eyes pushed out. "You must listen to me. We must know the truth!"

Sobs rose and choked as Abba released my face and sat back on his cushion with a thud. I looked at Ima who hadn't moved, her eyes still downcast, hands folded on her lap.

I struggled to speak as deep sobs interrupted my words.

"Abba …. Ima ….. I …. never disappoint you." I realized immediately the irony of my words as the look of disappointment on Abba's face could not be more apparent.

"Abba, please," I cried. "The baby, it is not Joseph's. It is not any man's."

The words coming out of my mouth seemed suddenly as absurd to me as they must have sounded to them.

"I was visited by an angel. The baby is God's child."

Ima shot a look at Abba.

"Joachim, is it possible? Is this what was meant?" she asked.

"Don't be ridiculous, Anah," he hissed back. "Do you realize what she's saying? She's claiming that the child is the Messiah."

I burst into tears and ran to my mattress at the back of the house. I climbed under the blanket and covered my head.

"What will we do Joachim?" Ima asked. "We are already humiliated by rumors. What will people think?"

I bit my lip and waited for Abba's response. He had said so little on the matter until now. Just one word from him; I just wanted to know that he would protect me.

"I will talk to the village elders. They will know what to do," he said.

I rested fitfully that night. Ima sobbed quietly, awakening frequently, startled by her dreams. Abba knelt by candlelight crying out to the God he loved, the God who had deserted him.

Dawn broke cruelly. No heralding the sun today. Only irate shouts called forth the morning. Ima ran to me while Abba pulled on his robes hastily to see what commotion had arrived at our door. Even the climbing vines retreated as the only fragrance wafting through the windows was of parched ground and the stale smell of men up all night. A group had gathered outside and pounded with sticks on the door, the walls, the ground.

"What's happening, Ima?" I asked fearfully.

She held me tighter, "I don't know, Mary. Abba will find out."

"Who is there? What do you want?" Abba asked as he reached the door.

"Joachim, you must let us in!" It was Gad, the *Rabbi*.

"Gad, why are you here so early? What do you want from us at this hour?" asked Abba.

We sensed the crowd getting bigger as the mumbles of female voices joined the men and way in the back, someone bellowed, "Stone her!"

Five

I screamed and clung to Ima, rigid. The pounding on the door increased and Abba stood motionless, not knowing what to do.

"Let us in or we'll knock the door down, Joachim!" one of the men shouted.

"This is out of your hands now," cried another.

"Enough!" Gad spoke again.

I had known him my whole life; a learned man, a *Pharisee*. He upheld the Jewish law in Nazareth; every word drew respect.

"Send your women home," he commanded the men who surrounded him.

Abba unlocked the door as the men started battering.

"Stop! Please stop! We want no trouble here, Gad," Abba pleaded but was met with coldness.

I had nowhere to run. The grotto would not protect me now. Many of these men had helped Abba build our house. They knew every nook.

"Wait outside," Gad commanded the village men gruffly.

Only two from the synagogue entered the house with him. They each found a cushion and motioned for us to sit. I nestled into Ima's arms. They wore the black robes of the synagogue, their head and shoulders draped clumsily with the prayer shawl as though they had dressed hurriedly. Their eyes were bloodshot from lack of sleep, faces drawn from hours of discussion. Gad, wise, discerning, compassionate waited to let hostility ease. I looked at him as he spoke to Abba. Would he be an advocate for me? Many times he had called on the children to include me and be kind when I was a child. Many times he had stood in my defense when blame was laid upon me, the smallest, the scapegoat. But this was no childish tiff. Would severity erase his memory?

"Talk is rampant." Gad sat up tall, intimidating in our small living room; voice echoing on stonewalls; the very house where he had celebrated my *Bat Mitzvah*, my birthdays, my birth.

"There is talk that Mary is pregnant. Joseph is nowhere to be found and now this soldier has violated our homes. He threatened to take a daughter from each household if you could not be found. You are fortunate, Mary. He passed out from his drunkenness and has gone. Now Nazareth is in danger."

He paused to give his words time to sink in.

"I have to ask you some questions," he went on. "You must answer honestly, do you understand?"

I nodded my head.

"Sit up and look at me," he commanded.

Ima pushed me upright and away from her. I looked up but heaviness forced my gaze to the floor.

"I will answer the best that I know how," I responded feebly.

"Are you pregnant?" he asked.

"Yes."

"Joseph has gone. Is the child his?"

"No."

"Does he know that you are pregnant?"

"Yes."

"And how did he respond?"

"He was very upset. I haven't seen him since."

Gad turned from me to my parents. "How long have you known?"

Abba spoke with a confidence I had not seen in him before.

"We found out last night but we too have heard the rumors. Mary is a good girl, Gad. Please consider what I am about to tell you, even though it may appear unlikely."

Gad leaned forward, imposing, jaw clenched.

Abba continued undeterred, "Mary had an encounter with a heavenly being. She believes that the child she is carrying is of the Holy Spirit and not of any man."

Gad pounded his fist on the floor and rose to his feet.

"Are you trying to tell me that Mary is the chosen one?" His voice bellowed as his eyebrows furrowed furiously.

Abba's confidence waned.

"I… I.. there's no other explanation. Mary has not been with a man…."

"Don't be a fool, Joachim."

31

He turned to me, frozen.

"This story is preposterous. Do you expect us to believe that God would choose you to bring us the Messiah, the One we have waited for? A poor child from Nazareth, betrothed to a carpenter. Are you mad?" Gad's voice rose in a crescendo of emotion. "If I accept this notion, we will be the talk of Galilee, of Israel. This must never be spoken of again."

The other men rose to join Gad as they consulted, pacing the floor.

"There are only two explanations," he finally stated. "Either you have committed adultery or you were raped and did not cry for help. Both are subject to death."

Justice hammered down hard. Mercy vanquished. Ima screamed and squeezed me tight. Abba cried out and stood between me and the men but they pushed him effortlessly aside.

"Please, Gad, my child, my child, I'll do anything, don't take my daughter."

His confidence now in shreds, tears ran helplessly down cheeks. Ima continued to scream as they grabbed me out of her arms. I fought to stay with her but could not struggle as Gad entwined my hair and pulled me upright to face him.

"This is a sad day for all of us, Mary," he growled. "You must cooperate."

I clung to his hands, trying to ease the pressure and pain. He released my hair while the other men tied my hands behind my back.

They half marched, half dragged me out of the house and through the streets. The men waiting outside, ears pressed to the door, surrounded me as I stumbled, trying to keep up. I shrank in my own eyes. Families gathered at

32

their doorways to watch the spectacle, ushering children back inside as I passed. We arrived quickly at the central courtyard where a crowd had gathered. I could hear the swish of water at the well and the sound of sobbing as my aunts looked on. The morning sun climbed, constant. Still not abandoned. Birds sang; song never changing.

"Poor Anah," the aunts uttered. "I can't imagine what she must be going through."

I realized that their tears were not for me, but for the family and the disgrace that they were enduring. My aunts had tolerated but never loved me. Their own daughters brought them great joy but I had been a sickly child from birth. I had screamed all day and night for the first months of my life and seemed to fall ill at the slightest touch of cold in the air. Ima struggled to keep me fed and content but I grew weaker and could not be consoled. She never tired of me though, remaining always patient, always kind. She kept me at home often, having to miss many family events and festivals for fear of illness. I finally outgrew the challenges of infancy but could never shake the stigma.

"The burden of this child on Anah must be worse than the shame of her barrenness," one of my aunts had whispered when I was no more than five years old.

Ima had overheard and took to her mattress weeping bitterly for the rest of the day while I played just a few feet away. I dared not approach her in case it was true.

Many hands shoved me to the ground where I lay curled up and trembling. Rough burlap was shoved hastily over my head. Everything had happened so fast but as I lay there with eyes covered, I melted into the nothingness. I resigned myself to death. There was nothing that Abba could do now, powerless against the laws of the Torah and the strength of our community. Confused, thoughts jumbled and then blank. My faith had been strong. Where was God now? My heart searched for something to hold onto.

I cried out in a whisper, *"My God, My God! Why have you forsaken me?"*

The crowd was agitated and arguments arose in different pockets of the group. As one argument subsided, another arose in its place in a swell of noise and disorder. Gad's voice rose steadily above the clamor as He began to read slowly and deliberately from the *Torah*.

"If, however, the charge is true and no proof of the young woman's virginity can be found, she shall be brought to the door of her father's house and there the men of her town shall stone her to death. She has done an outrageous thing in Israel by being promiscuous while still in her father's house. You must purge the evil from among you.[3]*"*

I had no defense; no one had believed my outrageous story. Maybe it would be better for everyone if I died. I had brought the grossest shame to my family. I could not see how a future was possible for my child and myself when my own community was rejecting me.

"Mary, you are sentenced to death by stoning for the crime of becoming pregnant before marriage."

Hope ebbed as I felt the men gather, each one an elder of the village, each one with daughters who I had played with my whole life. I had eaten in their homes, celebrated Pesach with them. Yet no loyalty or love can sway the integrity of the law. I was bound by it and subject to its commands, even though I knew that I was innocent. I heard the scrape of rocks being lifted off dusty ground as each man took his weapon. My hood shifted slightly allowing the light of dawn to break in. I saw the dirty, sandaled feet before me shifting from side to side, heavy linen tunics swaying gently around ankles.

Instructions were given for the procedure, stones thrown in unison until death. I shook in anticipation of the pain, hoping that it would not last long. Stones were lifted high as Gad recited prayers for justice. The prayers turned into chants as the men joined in; the rhythm mesmerizing, each one caught up in the moment. Women leaned out of their upper windows to watch the spectacle in the courtyard below. I closed my eyes in final surrender, not to them, but to the mystery.

A scream pierced the scene; chants splintered.

"It's Joseph!" she screamed again.

"What is he doing here?" asked another. "He left weeks ago."

My heart leaped. Joseph; my Joseph! Was it possible that he had returned?

His footsteps ran frantically through the streets and into the courtyard amidst shouts and shoves. Elders hovering over me, turned; the red sea parted.

"Stop! You must stop!" he shouted racing through the crowd, pushing men aside. He slid across the ground, feet dislodging rocks in their wake as he collided with me full pelt. He wrapped me up in his arms, knees tucked into belly. Burlap grazed skin, eyes locked, his sweat mingling with my tears as he held his cheek against mine.

"I *know*, Mary," he whispered. "I believe you."

Six

Shamed and bruised, I lay weakly across his knees as he bent over me, back to crowd. His tunic was rough and worn in parts but smelled of times past; times when the air was tinged with barley husks floating, and laughter rising to the midday sun. Calloused hands stroked my hair over and over while bearded lips whispered strength to my soul. I felt his muscles contract as he lifted me off the ground where my body should have lay, broken.

"Keep your eyes on me, Mary," he spoke to my heart.

One by one, stones fell to the ground as one by one, insults were picked up and hurled at our backs. Those who remained silent hung their heads and turned away. The bold, the audacious, they looked Joseph in the eye but still he walked, eyes forward. Arrowed words pierced me, "Sinner!"

"Wicked!"

"Better off dead!"

"Keep your eyes on me, Mary," Joseph repeated as the arrows bounced off his tender heart and fell to the ground.

My shame fell on his shoulders. The only explanation for Joseph's actions was that the child was his, conceived before marriage. Oh, the outrage! His dignity lay in shreds, his reputation stoned back there at the well. The crowd dissipated amidst murmurs of indignation and demands for justice.

We were soon alone. The air settled into peaceful respect; bird chirps waned in compassion as we walked past trees bending gently in the soft breeze. We did not speak but our thoughts were interrupted by screams and wailing from Abba's house. The sound was desperate, desperate, worse than the animals when they were led to sacrifice. I cringed, sobbing. Joseph held me tighter. He pushed the door open, light flooding the room darkened by covered windows. I saw Abba and Ima kneeling, clothes shredded, hair ripped, skin torn. He laid me on a mat and pulled the shades off the windows. Abba and Ima jumped, faces wild with grief, then confusion, then joy. Joy erupting.

"Joachim! The Lord has heard our prayers!" she screamed.

Abba fell to his knees, engulfed in tears. Joseph stood stoically in the corner, arms folded in front, watching the reunion, giving space.

"Come now," he finally entered the scene. "Joachim, this is not over yet. Please, leave Mary with her mother. We must talk."

Ima sat beside me singing softly and wiping my brow; hot with fever. Wrists grazed from rope burns and clumps of hair missing from my throbbing head. She covered me with a blanket when I shook with cold, and fed me drops of broth.

"Amazing grace," she whispered.

I drifted. First the darkness drew me into nothing, then the light pierced my eyes, swollen, sore; pulling me into awareness, into pain and I would pray for the darkness to come again. Abba entered and washed, tending his self-inflicted wounds. It was no more than an hour before Gad and the elders returned to the house. Abba would not let them in, but led them up the stairs to the roof where they baked in the ever-circling sun.

"I will take them wine," Ima spoke. "Lie still, Mary, I will not be long."

She smoothed her hair, replacing her tunic, and then hurried out of the house with the goblets and a platter of bread and fruit. My breathing increased as she disappeared; heart racing. I did not want to be left alone. I jumped as I heard the platter crash to the floor. Gad shouted at her; Abba's voice rose in defense. Joseph calmed them and sent Ima crying back to me. I sat up, suddenly alert and ready to run. Voices raised now, I shuffled closer to the window to listen. Ima stumbled through the door, locking it behind her. She did not come to me but busied herself with baskets of food that did not need to be rearranged.

"You have undermined the authority of the synagogue, Joseph. Your intrusion at the stoning puts you in contempt of the Torah. We will have to consider your punishment, and Mary's sentence is still under consideration," stated Gad.

"Rabbi," said Joseph. "You know me. I have attended

synagogue every week since birth. I have followed your teachings and upheld the law. I am a hard working man, not prone to rebellion or outbursts of any nature. And Mary, she is innocent. I know that her story is incredible; I didn't believe it myself at first and for many weeks I too could only see her sin and the need for justification."

"What are you saying, Joseph?" asked one of the elders. "You have both now confessed that the child is not yours. You cannot possibly consider marrying her. Doing so would place all the blame for this child on you. Are you not in agreement with us?"

"According to the law, yes. But is the law not also subject to God? He came to me in a vision. This is his work."

"Your words make no sense, Joseph. Why would God defy His own word? We must uphold His righteousness. Generations of our people have worshipped God through obedience to these laws and now you, a carpenter, have the audacity to tell us that God has changed His mind?"

Spit flew, tempers flared, elders seethed.

"No, Teacher. I do not dare to instruct you on the Word of God. All I know is that Mary is pregnant but not by man and surely not by me. I do not know what God wants or what he is doing. His only message to me was that I was not to be afraid to take her as my wife and that the child was conceived of the Holy Spirit."

Joseph spoke with humility and left the elders speechless.

"We must take all this before the counsel," said Gad. "We will reconvene in a week for trial."

He paused, the silence heavy with mistrust.

"Do you comprehend the cost if you choose to proceed with the marriage?" he went on. "Why don't you just divorce her quietly?"

"The only cost is to my dignity. The cost of disobeying God is far greater," Joseph replied resolutely.

"Then you must pray that God visits us too Joseph," Gad responded.

Joseph stood as the men rose and left. Abba had been silent through the whole interaction after Ima left. He faced Joseph and put his old, crooked hands on his shoulders.

"May God be with you, Joseph. I do not understand why God would visit us in this way," his voice cracked.

"I do not understand either, Joachim, but we must follow Him at all costs. You have been devoted to God and to the synagogue. He will not abandon you now."

For as long as I could remember, Abba had served in the synagogue. He rose early each morning to sweep the steps, and sang the songs of the Torah while he worked. On the *Sabbath*, he was the first one to arrive and the last one to leave. His devotion was unparalleled but he never required recognition. His voice was not sought after and his opinion was of little consequence; never asked for, and never offered. As a child, when Ima sent me outside to play, I would often search for Abba and find him praying in the synagogue. I had to be discreet and had found a small alcove in the corner where I fit perfectly and was partially hidden by a half wall to the right. I would imitate his posture and try to replicate the mumbled prayers as he cried out to God. His shoulders shook as he wept; his hands, outstretched, caught his tears. It was beautiful and although he was a man of very few words, his love of God had a profound impact upon my life. As I grew older and took on more responsibility in the home, I sometimes found myself alone and would recite the prayers and scriptures that I had memorized. When my tasks were done, I would kneel as Abba knelt and worship with the same love that I had seen in him. I knew God personally; at times the air would become so heavy with His presence that I could not stand or speak. I never asked for anything in those moments but the time and space to be with Him. For all the joy and laughter and fun that we experienced together in Nazareth, my greatest delight was found in those moments of breathtaking beauty. I looked for ways to serve and pour out this love that had filled my heart. I loved to visit the elderly women in our village. I would take them a spare loaf of bread and sit talking to them for hours, listening to their stories. I also spent much time taking care of the children. I sat with them at every opportunity, singing the songs that my grandmother, my *savta*, sang to me when I was very little. I loved to tell stories interwoven with lessons whenever I could. The children hung on every word and wrestled each other to sit on my lap. It was a rich life, never lonely.

Joseph did not visit me again. Abba said that it was best if we stayed apart until after the trial. Ima kept me in the house and no one came. I was crushed. Judgment had passed and I felt dreadfully misunderstood. I cried day after day. My only comfort was in the psalms of David and I fought to keep my mind at peace. I longed to explain myself and yet what explanation could I give that would not subject me to more humiliation and further question my sanity? Ima tried to comfort me but I withdrew to my bed or sat quietly grinding flour. After several days she stopped her attempts at talking, just pausing occasionally to kiss my forehead or wipe a tear from my eye.

Abba had always been a safe place, always affirming; understanding. Now, the weight pressing in started to tear us apart. I could not speak to him and neither did he seek to draw out my heart. A tender look or a hand laid on my head reassured me of his love, but my heart longed for affirmation as it strained under the voice of accusation and fear.

I thought often of Joseph in those lonely days. I missed him terribly. All the anticipation of our upcoming marriage had evaporated and the thought of losing him was as grievous to me as the difficulty that this pregnancy had brought upon me. His words of confidence had reignited my hope and faith and yet had come with no explanation. I longed for him to hold me again and to tell me what he knew and how. Had the angel also visited him? I had replayed my own encounter over and over in those first few weeks, wondering many times if I had dreamed or imagined it. Only when there was evidence of the pregnancy did I truly believe it. Even then, the fear of my circumstances often threatened to overwhelm the truth and it was easier to live under the perceived curse than to rise above it. My mind wandered back to that fateful day; the recollection sifting into my memory, bittersweet.

Seven

There had been no warning, no change in atmosphere or heart that would indicate that something momentous might take place. The morning had been uneventful except for threat of rain in the overcast skies that matched my mood. I was not proud of my range of emotions, longing to be more consistent but yielding to the struggle more often than not. Abba had left early and would not return until evening. Ima had taken to the field intending, I'm sure, to stay clear of me. I groaned, unable to sleep but not wanting to rise. Nothing stirred within me. I called out to God.

"I'm sorry! I'm sorry for the way I am."

Peace did not flood and my mind wondered over my

wretchedness. Abba always said that I thought too much. Perhaps, but I didn't know how to stop the onslaught once it began. I finally rose.

"I will sweep!" I spoke to the walls and to the broom in frustration. Tears slid down my face and I did not know why.

Slowly, as I worked the ache subsided. The tears dried. I had no reason for them, no excuse. In an effort to find gladness, I recalled the times that God had delivered my ancestors and I thanked Him. It was difficult to imagine that life could get better as the threat of disaster was always on the horizon, but my people were resilient in hope. Often it seemed like a mere thread and yet it wove its way through history unbound and indestructible.

Alone in the house I swept and sang the murmured praises of a heart tossed; the room listlessly grey. The remains of breakfast sat cold and my stomach growled with hunger. I ate what I could and then returned to finish my chores. As I squatted down to sweep a pile of dust in the corner, I was startled by intense heat behind me. I stumbled forward; looking up to see flames blazing fiercely along the walls, raging fire of red and brilliance. Screaming, I dropped the brush, falling to the floor as I spun around. My heart galloped; I could not think. Flames licked my face and charged my hands. I gasped for breath as I tried to back away along the wall, searching desperately for the door. A piercing beam shot through the blaze and pinned me to the wall as the air before me burst open in a shower of splintering light. The heat began to subside and I realized that the house and my face were not burning up. Panic stricken I sat motionless. The flames backed away and began to gather as though they were alive. The room burst with the presence of one

ushered in from the throne. He stood silent, stoic. I dared
not move. I hardly dared breath. He shifted his weight and
the earth groaned. He clenched, then unclenched his hands
as he pulled his elbows back and flexed shoulders covered
in simple linen, torn and tattered. Dark skin; he licked his
lips and reached for his beard, shorn close. He leaned; arms
crossed, hand on rugged chin deep in thought as he surveyed the sparse room. Studded leather bracelets wrapped
his forearms and he pulled a knife from its pouch. I drew
in breath, captivated, waiting. It darted, spinning upwards,
then caught deftly in his hand, again and again. The flames
continued their dance, sometimes raging upwards, deafening, sometimes spiraling around. He did not look at me.
His lips moved in silent conversation, head cocked to listen.
He showed no sense of urgency. I waited. Flames erupted,
sound of thunder. I stifled a scream; hands clenched over
open mouth. Now he sees me. Eyes, deep onyx set in whites
of snow; eyes that told a thousand stories connected with
mine, a story of one. His eyes widened, incredulous and
then narrowed, questioning. Wind blew; flames billowed.
He waited more, listening, searching. Mighty breath of God
drew in; he shook his head in disbelief, tousled curls tossed,
back and forth. He peered into the world beyond and then
fell to one knee, rock like. Head hung and palms stretched
out low, fingers thick as branches, spread and marked with
veins of blood coursing. Gold signet etched with splendor.
Transfixed on the floor. I waited still.

He lifted his face and drew it ever so slightly closer to
mine, probing, then nodding, knowing. He rose to his feet,
I cowered. He twisted, looking back over his shoulder at the
row of vessels behind him. He reached for water, splashing
it over his face and exposing a tattoo that stretched from

his jaw, down his thick neck and wove around his bicep. A deep, fresh scar along his forearm and the wounds of his face indicated that he was a warrior. The straps of his armor creaked under the strain of movement. He looked wind swept, as though his journey here had been fraught with danger and haste; sweat beaded across his temple. His armor was simple, crude even, especially compared with the sword, exquisite, that hung by his side; edged with raw power and hailed straight from Heaven, that much I knew. My body shook, fear dripped across my brow and over trembling lips.

He turned away from me suddenly, feet planted solid, and reached into the world beyond. The room split apart once again and light flooded, a light so magnificent that the fire paled in comparison. The warrior heaved with all his might to usher in a creature so breathtaking that in his presence I was no longer aware of my surroundings. My eyes that should have been blinded by such a light were transformed to see into another dimension.

Billowing cloth of silk and gold cascaded as the angel alighted from Kingdom. The sound of multiple wings striking air caused me to cover my ears. Each wing span the size of a man and pure platinum, etched with jewels. They dripped with oil. His feet landed barefoot before me, skin translucent. He folded his wings as he unfolded his arms and reached for me. I shuddered, retreating, eyes darting between the abundance of him, and the immensity of Warrior, standing by his side.

"Greetings, you who are highly favored! The Lord is with you.[4]*"*

I jolted back at the sound of his voice, tears finally released as my soul shook under the reverberation of each word and I *wondered what kind of greeting this might be*[5]. He did not take his eyes off me and I calmed in the silence of his gaze.

"Do not be afraid, Mary, you have found favor with God. You will be with child and give birth to a son, and you are to give him the name Jesus. He will be great and will be called the Son of the Most High. The Lord God will give him the throne of his father David and he will reign over the house of Jacob forever; his kingdom will never end.[6]*"*

His voice, gentle now, a waterfall. I watched the words come out of his mouth. They moved and joined together creating colors and images that I did not understand. He waited, allowing me to process what I was seeing, what I had heard. He shifted, playing with the images that formed between us, moving them this way and that. The pictures suddenly evaporated and I returned with a start to the sight of him standing before me. His face shimmered, without definite form but exuding kindness; his hair like the sky during the last brilliant display of sunset; ears set with diamonds, and thick belt of purist gold that could circle two men. He dazzled in brightest white. My heart began to steady, the surge of fire replaced with awe of holiness.

"How will this be," I asked, *"since I am a virgin?*[7]*"*

Warrior angel stared intently through the ceiling, agitated. My voice distracted him and he turned quickly to look at me, full of haste now. Light of love increased through the other and I found peace in his steel eyes. He was unperturbed. Smiling, he leaned closer, lowering his voice.

"The Holy Spirit will come upon you. The power of the Most High will over shadow you. So the holy one to be born will be called the Son of God.[8]*"*

Was I dreaming? But I could smell his honey breath and I knew that I could not be asleep. I saw again the picture that his words created and I reached out to touch. I saw a terrible darkness and then *the curtain from the temple was torn in two from top to bottom*[9]. Light erupted in such violence that darkness fled. A man emerged through the veil. His body that had been battered and pierced restored with each step. His smile grew as his walk turned to a run. He passed a tomb throwing aside the rock that barricaded it. Death scurried out defeated. He ran for many days, his joy growing, and then he ascended victoriously with shouts of glory into eternity.

The angel continued, *"Even Elizabeth your relative is going to have a child in her old age, and she who was said to be barren is in her sixth month. For nothing is impossible with God.*[10]*"*

Unbelievable! Elizabeth! My aunt. But she was so old. I sat, stunned, mouth gaping. I had heard of Elizabeth, pious and distant. Talk of her pained my mother but I did not know why. I had never met her; strange since our family was loyal and blood ran thick. We made our pilgrimage to Jerusalem often, passing their house but never venturing there. Abba carried a deep sadness over his sister but Ima's wound ran deeper still and time had not healed.

The angel's words were breathtaking. Was it possible that I had been chosen to birth the Messiah? My mind ran back over the events of the morning.

Prophets and kings had spoken of the One, and of the virgin who would carry him, and scriptures documented the stories that led to this. But, me? My head shook side-to-side in disbelief, but if Elizabeth was pregnant, then the impossible had happened; the story was already unfolding.

I had not moved. My gaze fixed on hands wringing. Warrior Angel became impatient as I pondered racing thoughts. I lifted my eyes to Steel Blue as he reached towards me again. His fingers ran with oil. As he poured it lavishly over my brow. It streamed over my cheeks and my heart burned with the overwhelming presence of unconditional and undeserved love.

"I am the Lord's servant," I whispered, as oil and tears ran down my neck. *"May it be to me as you have said.*[11]*"*

His eyes were tender and filled with compassion as he pressed his hand over my head. I leaned forward, accepting, and then his wings unfurled with an almighty crack and he was gone.

Warrior stepped in front of me, eyes dark as storm. His gaze bore deep; then weathered face creased as he laughed, explosive. He helped me to my feet, then spiraled away and disappeared. A surge of wind accompanied his exit as the flames extinguished in a flash.

I was left alone once again. The room seemed dull and lifeless compared to the awe of kingdom light. I looked around, not sure what to do next, so I picked up my broom and continued to sweep.

Eight

Joseph and I were both descendents of King David, Israel's greatest. Joseph's ancestry traced back through royal line, mine did not, although the decline from royalty was stark and Joseph was wise to keep the knowledge to himself. He worked tirelessly hard. His father had taught him a good trade and he was a skilled carpenter. He had lived alone at the edge of Nazareth for as long as I could remember but he was always available to anyone in need. The village leaned heavily on him in times of crisis. His quiet ways brought peace and confidence and drew respect from the men. He was adept with tools and knew the land well. He laughed often and with kindness but carried the scars of sadness behind his eyes. He was well loved but little known. He did not involve himself in issues of politics or debates of religious law, preferring instead to retreat to work, or to teach the children a new game at the well. Children hung on his arms and off every word. Gentleness poured.

One morning when I had followed Abba into the synagogue I saw that Joseph was there, kneeling at the front. I was curious as there was rarely anyone but Abba in the synagogue at this time of day. The high walls and stone columns dwarfed the lonely figure. I quickly hid in my little alcove and watched as Abba swept the stone platform seating that skirted the walls. The Torah scrolls were hidden in the ark at the front with the eternal flame blazing overhead, casting a gentle glow on the earthen floor below. Joseph knelt before the raised platform; head hung low. He wept quietly, heart breaking. It was known that he had lost his wife and child some years before and had not remarried. He never spoke of what happened but carried the monument to his anguish daily. Abba swept this way and that, slowly making his way towards the front and finally approaching Joseph. Tender hand of father's love rested on his shoulder, drawing his face upwards, tears glistening in candlelight.

"Come, my son," Abba said softly. "Your pain will not release you until you release it."

Joseph shook with sobs.

"You are living on the edge of your suffering, Joseph," Abba counseled. "You must find a way to push through the pain to the deeper place where only God is found. There you will find your healing."

"I'm afraid that the pain will be much greater there?" asked Joseph.

"Perhaps," replied Abba. "But that is also where love

resides and there is no fear in love. What are you afraid of, Joseph?"

"I am afraid of being swallowed up by shame, Joachim."

Silence followed, heavy laden. I wept silently behind them both, as compassion filled my spirit. It was difficult to understand their conversation as I was still a child, but the presence of God fell into the room and I was moved to a deep place that I had not known before. Finally, Joseph spoke; his voice barely audible as he turned to face my father.

"It was my fault," he spoke with despair. "I watched them die and I could do nothing to save them. I watched my child die."

Pain throbbed through the room as Abba wrapped his arms around him. I watched as he lifted his head to Heaven; tears rolled down his cheeks and onto Joseph's head. I left quickly, regretting my curiosity. It was uncommon to see a man cry, to see him in weakness.

Joseph spoke often with Abba. I watched him whenever he came to the house but he never looked at me. I served them quietly, always listening. Ima would scold me when I was younger and send me out to play. As I got older, I looked forward to Joseph's visits. Abba had taken him under his wing and he occasionally shared the *Shabbat* meal with us. They spoke of work and the latest news from Jerusalem. I never again saw any hint of the tears that I had seen at the synagogue, although his humility and wisdom impressed me. He carried great reverence for the Lord and yet much of his conversation with Abba carried a vein of doubt about his self-worth. He wrestled with this over and over and never seemed to come to any sort of conclusion. At first I pitied him because of his tears, but over time I grew to respect him. As the years passed, my heart would beat a little faster when I heard him approach our door. One evening after dinner, Abba rose and stretched, beckoning me to go with him.

"Come Mary, we will walk through the olive grove together. I have something I would like to discuss with you."

His invitation delighted me. Every word from Abba was precious and I craved his attention. I grabbed my shawl and followed him outside, through the alleys and up the hill. Soft leaves danced in moon bathed shadows as the sun gave a final wave on the horizon. I tucked my arm though his and drew in close. As a child I would clatter chatter on our evening walks. Mind filled with nonsense and everything, words cascading, ears listening, chuckles brimming over. Now my quest was for more of him. I silenced the clang of words in my head and waited for him to speak.

"What do you think of Joseph?" he asked me outright.

"Joseph?" My face reddened against my will and to my surprise. "Abba, what are you asking? I don't know how to answer your question."

"Joseph has come to me with a proposal, Mary. He would like to ask for your hand."

I was shocked. I hadn't expected to receive such a request. Joseph was older and although it was far from unusual for a man to ask for the hand of a girl much younger, I would not have imagined that he would see anything worth pursuing in me.

"What did you tell him?"

"I gave him my consent but told him that I would like to discuss the matter with you first."

Marriages were largely arranged and the woman's opinion was rarely consulted. I felt honored.

"Mary, I trust and respect Joseph but your happiness is

of great importance to me. What are your thoughts on the matter?"

"I like Joseph very much," I replied cautiously. "And I trust you Abba."

We walked silently for a while, enjoying the cool breeze and the smells of impending summer.

"Then what is your hesitation? There is a hesitation, isn't there?"

I nodded my head, not sure what to say without exposing what I knew.

"Joseph seems to be lost somehow, like he carries a wound that won't heal, like he doesn't know who he is. I have heard the way that he talks. I want a man who is strong and capable, who can protect me."

Abba turned to look at me, searching my innocent eyes.

"My child, you must not equate vulnerability with weakness. Joseph's brokenness prepares the way for great courage."

He paused and then continued almost as though he were talking to himself.

"Perhaps we are too quick to define strength. Is it the ability to conquer, to be impregnable, to assert oneself? If that is the case then Herod shows great strength, and yet he is clearly a man plagued by weakness. Force of strength does not make a person powerful. Sometimes the lowest among us shows the greatest strength…"

His voice trailed off and his attention returned to me.

"It is always our choice how we respond to another. *A powerful person's choice to love will stand, no matter what the other person says or does*[12]. Will you approach Joseph in fear or in love? Fear says, 'I only see your weakness and therefore I cannot love you.' "

I slept very little that night. The ability to love without reservation, without condition, seemed impossible to achieve; I realized that fear was the driving force in most of my choices and relationships.

"Adonai," I called out in whispered prayer. "Help me to choose the right way. I am overcome with fear."

I awoke the next morning, no more certain of my course and no less fearful of it. Spirit said yes but heart urged resistance, unnerving fear or unwavering trust.

"I am yours, Lord."

I spoke my commitment and resolved in my heart to be obedient to His will, "I choose love."

A month later, Joseph arrived at our house for an elaborate meal. There was great excitement as I had finally accepted his offer of marriage and the betrothal ceremony was a vital tradition. Our house was transformed from a simple home to a feast of colors, food and friends. Ima draped fabric to cover the drab walls and hung clusters of fragrant flowers from the ceiling. Lamps shone brightly as evening fell and our guests arrived. I sat waiting at the head of a large table that filled the room, and my family and friends took their seats; children lined the walls giggling in anticipation. My heart surged as I heard Joseph approach and I knew with certainty that I had made the right decision. Gad entered first, his head covered with the prayer shawl and the straps of the *tefallin* hanging as they wove around his arm and fingers. These small boxes containing verses of the Torah commanded reverence among us and a hush fell over the room. We waited silently as the door opened and Joseph entered, hair slick with anointing oil, white linen robes freshly sewn. Abba and Ima greeted him warmly and they stood before Gad while he recited scriptures and spoke of the legalities of the agreement. I looked expectantly at Joseph and waited as the contract was drawn up and the scribe wrote the terms on the *ketubah*. Joseph laid the document out before me; decorated with covenant symbols. He looked deeply into my eyes as he spoke. I felt the room fade and the presence of everyone else in the room disappear as I met his eyes. He drew near; close enough that I could inhale his breath.

"I choose you, Mary," his voice broke to a whisper as he held the cup of wine.

A drink from the cup would signify that I had accepted his proposal and we would be betrothed. Even though it may be several years before we were married, the betrothal was binding. Our hands shook as he passed the cup to me. As our fingers touched, my body burned, face flushed. His words resonated through my soul, 'I choose you.' I had never heard the groom state those words at a betrothal, even though each action and the proposal itself implied it.

"I am chosen," I whispered to myself. I took a sip of wine and the room erupted in shouts and laughter. Music struck and people spilled dancing into the streets. Joseph reached for my hand, fingers touched, eyes knowing; then he was whisked away to celebrate while I remained to savor the sweetness of love promised.

Nine

What would happen now? What could happen? Joseph had rescued me. He said that he believed me but would he still marry me? Our betrothal meant nothing now; this pregnancy gave him every right to divorce me and our culture pressed him to do so.

We only had days left until the trial and I knew that my situation did not look good; perhaps even worse than before. Tempers flared in the village. Scorn brewed; even if a resolution could be found, was there any way to salvage our lives? Could there be any return to those happy days when we used to sing, all the children together at my grandmother's house. Savta was a wise, proud woman. She was revered among women but loved by children. She always baked treats and we would crowd into her home every week to recite the stories of our ancestors. She made up songs so we could remember the facts. She smiled at each one and called us by name. "Sit up tall, you are an Israelite!" she scolded with a twinkle in her eye. "Straighten that tunic, Yoav. Calm that unruly hair, Haddy." She opened up a world of promise. She taught us that each one was special. She did not single me out with favor but I was certain of her love. Children swaying in song; arm-in-arm, joined by smiles. All of it just memories now, nothing would be the same again.

"Come, Mary," Abba had returned home and spoke softly. "You must eat. Come and sit with me."

I pushed the heaviness out of my way as I approached him. He handed me a bowl of broth and I dipped my bread, letting the savory juice wash down my throat and revive.

"It is good that you stay home, Mary. The people are in shock, they are confused. People rarely behave well under times of stress. You must try to see this through their eyes."

"But if I see things their way then I should be stoned, I should be dead," I responded angrily. "They do not want to believe the truth, they don't even want to hear it."

I pushed disheveled hair from my face. Eyes swollen and face splotched from too much sadness.

"That is not what I mean, Mary. I am talking about compassion, about forgiveness. You know the truth, but the truth has not settled into their hearts and may never. I am talking about your freedom to love them regardless of their response to you. See the situation from their perspective and then pray for them. If you will not forgive them, then bitterness can creep in and rob you of your freedom."

His words were weighty. They were too much for me.

The pain and the rejection were overwhelming. It was all that I could see and feel.

"Joseph is working on the situation. You must trust God. Your only position of strength is in trust. Lay your heart bare, Mary. These are days of destiny and you hold them in your hands."

I pulled out my mat, lay down and wept. I wondered if I had made the right decision? My choice was tearing my family, my love and my community apart. Would God save me now? Was this going according to plan? I woke up when night had already fallen and the darkness of the third nightwatch was underway. I heard voices in the front of the house and stayed where I was so that I didn't disturb them. My mouth and throat were dry and my arm was numb from laying on it while I slept. My mattress was pushed up against the back wall deep in the shadows. The soft glow of candles flickered by the door.

I rolled over and strained to hear who was with my parents. I almost called out when I realized that Savta was there. She was one of my favorite people, always gentle, always loving, but something about the tone of conversation stopped me from saying anything. Their voices were grave.

"Joachim," Savta said, "you must listen to reason. Dinah is a gifted midwife. I have spoken to her in length and she has reassured me that she can take care of this."

Abba sighed and Ima shifted to take his hand. Savta spoke again. Her voice calm, convincing.

"The disgrace that Mary has brought to your household and to our family is incomprehensible. The implications will outlast you my son. Already your business is suffering. Anah, I have seen the pain in your eyes when you meet the women at the well. And what of Mary, Joachim? Does she not have the right to a life without the pain and struggle that this pregnancy has brought on her? I know that she thinks that this is God's work but no one believes her. She was almost killed. At best she will be branded for life. What purpose will that serve?" She paused for a moment as her words sank into the earth. "Family, you know that I only want the best for us all. This situation can be easily resolved and we must consider the good of everyone involved. It is currently of little consequence, but if we allow it to come forth it will only bring shame and division and will be the subject of ridicule and rejection."

A new voice spoke into the conversation; a voice that pierced the pervading darkness. I rolled over silently to reposition. Joseph spoke steady and quiet. I strained to hear.

"Savta," Joseph said kindly. "May I call you Savta, for I already feel that I am a part of this family? Joachim has embraced me as his son, and my love for Mary runs deep. This situation is indeed a solemn one and I cannot deny the logic of your words. How simple it would be to eliminate this so that we can all go back to the lives we know and love."

Savta shifted on her seat, leaning back and folding her hands triumphantly on her lap. She turned to Dinah.

"Leave instructions with Anah. She will see to the details and will expect your return in two days."

Mumbled whispers as Abba and Joseph spoke quietly. Savta ruled. She turned to Ima.

"Dinah will leave a concoction of herbal remedies that will start the contractions. Hopefully nothing more will be needed but Dinah will return to see that it is expelled. If it is not, a small course of action will be necessary to complete the procedure. In two days this will all be over."

The group rose quickly and disbanded, leaving the room

eerily quiet. Abba and Ima moved silently past me to their mattresses. Adrenaline coursed. I kept my breathing steady so that they would think I was still sleeping but there was no more sleep for me that night; my mind raced. Was it possible that this could all be over in two days? Relief washed over me, but what of the child? I quickly pushed the thoughts away. I was confused and wrestled in conflict all night long. There was something inside that wanted to fight, something that was willing to endure anything to protect my child. And yet those who were my protectors were speaking of this matter easily and without regret. Surely I could trust them to make the right decision.

I tried to find peace, to find God but I tossed and turned. Finally, just as dawn began to break and I drifted in and out of consciousness, a memory long forgotten wove through my dreams.

I was close to the age of my Bat Mitzvah. We were returning from Jerusalem for our annual visit to the temple for Passover, an important pilgrimage. Each night we set up camp to eat and rest as the journey was long on foot.

I was in our tent, filled with the delights of the last six days. I hummed quietly to myself when I heard voices whispering in the tent next to mine. I recognized the voice of Dvora, the young midwife from our village, and her mother.

"It was terrible. I cannot get the sight out of my mind," Dvora's voice shook as she spoke.

"Whatever happened?" asked her mother.

"I met the midwife from Jerusalem, her name is Dinah," Dvora began. "She is very experienced. I was honored that she would speak with me as I wanted to learn more. We met in her home and talked while she made sweet bread and tea. Suddenly, there was banging on the door and a woman called out 'Dinah, come quickly. My daughter! You must come quickly!'

"Dinah jumped up, her face pale. She grabbed a bag that was sitting by the door and turned to me, her voice stern, "Return to your people immediately."

"I was curious so I jumped up after she left and followed her, hiding behind the corners of buildings. I saw her disappear into a house where there was a terrible groaning, wild and frantic. I almost ran away but I knew that this was something different. I was ambitious, naïve. I ran to the house and into the alley. Climbing the stairs I could just reach the window. I peered in; a young woman was laid out on the mat moaning in pain. She was past the first stage of pregnancy. I heard the woman who had come for Dinah as she spoke and sobbed simultaneously:

'I did everything you told me but it isn't working, can you save her?'

"Dinah opened her bag and went to work, barking instructions as she went, 'Put this in her mouth to stop her screaming.'

"She knelt before the woman on the mat whose eyes opened wide with pain but her mother pushed a cloth in her mouth to muffle the screams. Dinah worked until a gush poured. The woman on the mat passed out, her head fell to one side and the cloth fell to the ground. Her mother collapsed; sweat dripping. She pushed herself backwards, dislodging clods of dirt as she dug heels into floor. She cowered against the wall, turning her head away; fists to eyes.

" 'What have we done?' she moaned.

"Dinah continued and I watched in revulsion as she took forceps, scissors, clamps, and started to dismember tiny life.

" 'Quickly, you must help now,' she instructed the mother.

'Lift her head and try to rouse her. She has lost a lot of blood.'

"The unearthly tension in the room leaked out of the window and choked. The smells mingled with imminently approaching death. I spun away, heart pounding. Faint with shock I gasped in horror as all fell silent except for the first and last infant cry."

Ten

I arose to the smell of breakfast cooking and took my seat, heart heavy. My body hurt, eyes dry from lack of sleep. I stared into the pot and watched the water bubble gently. Ima was quiet. Usually we chatted and planned the day but the room was thick with awkward silence. I saw the packages of herbs on the floor by the bags of grain.

"Ima," I choked, hands shaking. "Ima, those packages; I can't…"

She interrupted before I could finish my sentence.

"Hush now child. Joseph is on his way to see you. You must eat and be ready when he arrives." She tried to smile.

I ate and dressed quickly, anxious about a visit from

Joseph. What would I say, what could I do? I was determined but how would I convince him?

"Where is Abba?" I asked.

"He left early to pray. He will be home soon."

Within minutes, Abba and Joseph arrived together. I suddenly felt outnumbered, as though the whole world was against me, against my son. Was I the only one whose love he would know? Abba scurried into the room and embraced Ima.

"Gather her belongings, Anah. We don't have much time; they must be on their way soon."

Ima wiped her eyes and hurried to pack my clothes and a meal. Joseph walked in tall; his height suddenly imposing and I cowered before him. His tunic billowed and I looked away as he knelt before me.

"Do not be afraid, Mary. We must leave this house but you will return. Say goodbye to your abba and ima. Hurry now." His tone was gentle and he took my chin in his hands.

I relaxed in his touch, but was still bewildered. They didn't know that I had heard their conversation last night.

"Where are we going, Joseph? I, I must tell you something," I stammered.

"What is it, Mary?" he asked as he rose to take the sack from Ima.

"The baby." Tears welled up in my eyes and spilled over onto my cheeks. "The baby..."

It was all I could get out. Joseph took my hand and pulled me up. He leaned forward so that our eyes were level.

"No one will hurt my son," he spoke confidently. "I will protect you and this child with my life. I claim him as my own."

Relief tumbled over me once again but this time it was

not for me. Abba and Ima took me in their arms and prayed blessings for safety. They kissed me goodbye and before I could blink, Joseph was leading me on the back of a donkey out of Nazareth towards the main travel route.

"Where are we going, Joseph?" I finally dared ask.

"You will stay with your cousin, Elizabeth. You are no longer safe in Nazareth. She is with child too and will bring you much comfort."

I didn't know Elizabeth, but my father spoke fondly of her. Feelings of relief and anticipation jostled with waves of anxiety as we turned from all I had known.

The journey was long and the sun beat down on us. For four days we traveled. My lack of sleep the night before left me weary and it was difficult to get comfortable. My head nodded frequently, heavy with exhaustion, and more than once Joseph had to catch me before I slid off the donkey. The road was empty. There was no reason for people to travel to Jerusalem at this time of year, and the farmers were busy with their fields. The soldiers were training north and our only concern was bandits. Thankfully our days were uneventful and our nights were spent in towns. We hardly spoke. It was uncommon for a betrothed couple to spend any time together before the wedding and yet here we were alone; accusation plagued us and I could not shake the uneasy feeling that we had only tasted the enormity of what lay ahead. Joseph sang as we walked; the sound gave me comfort but they were not joyful songs. I wished for the songs of my childhood but those days were far behind me now. The smells of dried fruit that we had brought to snack on made me nauseous and I became weak with hunger.

As night began to fall on the fourth day, we arrived at the edge of a town much bigger than Nazareth. It was intimidating but I was glad for it; I hoped that my arrival would go unnoticed and I looked forward to being inconspicuous. It took a long time to find Elizabeth's house. The streets were a maze of three story houses and market stalls and we seemed to go around in circles. Lamps hung in doorways and made our way possible as the sun finally set behind us. A merchant who was tearing down his stall for the night pointed us in the right direction and just as I thought I could not take another step, we arrived. The house was nestled among other equally imposing structures that burst with the sounds of children playing and the aroma of dinner cooking. The donkey brayed and must have signaled our arrival as a small, wiry man ran out to meet us. He nodded and clapped his hands, flitting around, first shaking Joseph's hands, and then patting the donkey; directing it to the back of the house. He was an odd looking man but I was too tired to care. He motioned us towards the door.

"Come, Mary," Joseph encouraged. "I'm sure Elizabeth has a meal and a bed waiting," he said warmly.

The door opened before us and I was shocked at the sight of a woman even older than my father in the doorway. Her hair was grey, folds of skin wrinkled her face and she was visibly pregnant. She seemed to search around in the darkness even though I was standing before her. Her gaze was cool and she looked over my shoulder at Joseph and then back at me.

"Come in, Mary." She turned slightly to make room for me to pass through.

I responded timidly, "Thank you, thank you for letting me come."

As I spoke, Elizabeth bent double and clutched at her swollen abdomen. Joseph reached forward instinctively to catch her. She straightened, her face suddenly flushed with color, eyes bright.

"I'm fine, Joseph," she gasped between breaths as laughter took over and her body shook until tears poured down her face. She grasped the doorframe to keep herself steady. The man who had first greeted us came running around the corner. His arms flailed wildly as he tried to ascertain what had come over Elizabeth. She grabbed his arm, her body still convulsing as she howled with laughter. She could barely speak as it took her breath away.

"Zechariah!" she finally exclaimed. "The baby…."

We all drew in closer as she slid down the doorpost, the laughter not easing. What about the baby? Zechariah gestured wildly again and pointed to her belly.

"The baby…. it leaped in my womb…. when Mary spoke… and I am filled with the most indescribable joy!"

By now she had slid further down onto the ground as though she was drunk. Neighbors were peering out of doorways to see what was the matter. Zechariah motioned for Joseph to help and they dragged her into the house and laid her on a mat. I followed them in and waited by the door. Elizabeth's behavior was disarming but I could not deny the familiar presence of God that fell over me as I entered.

The house was much grander than ours; white washed walls replaced the mud bricks of the poorer homes. Ornate furniture separated dining room and living area where colorful cloths, pillows and rugs beckoned guests warmly. The front of the house was large and open leaving plenty of space for small gatherings. The marble floor felt cool under my feet and I was embarrassed by the pile of dust that had already fallen off my shoes. I wondered how she ever kept it clean. Our floor of beaten earth was swept daily but never exposed the filth that accumulated on our feet. There was a separate area at the back of the room that housed the domestic animals through the winter; their breath and body heat warming the house at night. Two steps rose up to the raised platform where mattresses filled with wool were laid out for sleeping. Most of the houses we had passed had one or two more levels added above to accommodate children, but Elizabeth had never had any need for the space until now.

I waited nervously while the men attended to Elizabeth who was still overcome with laughter and showed no signs of stopping. Zechariah seemed perturbed but had not uttered a word. He left Elizabeth's side when it was apparent that nothing more could be done for her and busied himself with the pot of soup that was about to boil over. He motioned to us to sit. We found stools around a low table across from him. He just stared at us. We ate bowls of soup in silence while Elizabeth continued to stifle howls behind us, occasionally giving in to belly laughs.

"You must sleep now, Mary," Joseph finally said. "It has been a long week. Rest, and tomorrow I will leave."

I gripped his hand.

"Why must you leave me?" I asked.

"It is not appropriate for us to stay here together until we are married," he replied. "Tonight I will sleep on the roof. I will not leave until you are awake."

A mattress had been prepared for me in the corner of the platform and a large sheet was draped from the ceiling for privacy. I made my way to bed and slid into the blankets, not even aware of laying my head down. I awoke the next day when the sun was high and I heard Elizabeth grinding flour. She seemed a little more composed, chuckles only escaping now and then. I rubbed the sleep out of my eyes as I crossed the room, and sat down on the mat.

"Where is Joseph?" I asked, concerned that he may have left.

"He had to pick up supplies but will be back soon to eat before he leaves," she responded.

Elizabeth continued grinding the flour, her eyes searching my face while I looked around the room. I turned to look at her when the sound of the millstone ceased. Her eyes were still moist from the tears of laughter. She reached over to me and put her hand on my knee.

"Blessed are you among women, and blessed is the child you will bear!" she exclaimed. *"But why am I so favored, that the mother of my Lord should come to me?*[13]*"*

"I don't know," I responded. "I don't know why I have been chosen."

I waited a moment and then continued, "How can you be so sure, Elizabeth? No one else has believed me. I don't even know if Abba and Ima really believe me."

"As soon as the sound of your greeting reached my ears, the baby in my womb leaped for joy,[14]*"* she replied. "I had been getting worried as I had not felt him move. Fear was besetting me and all I had to cling to was the promise. It was spoken to my husband that our son would be filled with the Holy Spirit even before he was born. This is all as the angel told him. I don't understand it either, Mary, but there is no denying the miraculous work of God in both of our lives."

Her words strengthened and encouraged me. Her faith was certain and her joy was becoming contagious.

"Blessed is she who has believed that the Lord would fulfill his promises to her![15]*"* she stated boldly, my hands now clasped in hers.

I felt confusion melt away; the trauma of the last week faded as the presence of God filled the room.

"I'm bursting with God-news; I'm dancing the song of my Savior God," I declared. *"God took one look at me, and look what happened — I'm the most fortunate woman on earth! What God has done for me will never be forgotten, the God whose very name is holy, set apart from all others. His mercy flows in wave after wave on those who are in awe before him. He bared his arm and showed his strength, scattered the bluffing braggarts. He knocked tyrants off their high horses, pulled victims out of the mud. The starving poor sat down to a banquet; the callous rich were left out in the cold. He embraced his chosen child, Israel; he remembered and piled on the mercies, piled them high. It's exactly what he promised, beginning with Abraham and right up to now.*[16]*"*

We laughed and embraced, both of us filled with the excitement of our extraordinary pregnancies.

Eleven

The door swung open and Joseph stepped in, taking a seat beside me. I fetched a bowl of water and washed the dust off his feet, tending to his wounds from days of walking. I wished that he did not have to leave so soon. His face was haggard but his eyes were brighter and more beautiful than I had seen before. I felt safe with him as I had with Abba when I was a child and I used to climb onto his lap and curl up. The recollection brought comfort and I closed my eyes, remembering his voice as he rocked me to sleep. I dried Joseph's feet and rubbed ointment on them to soothe. I consoled myself that I was marrying a good man. Many of the girls had dreams of marrying a wealthy merchant or a distinguished priest. There were a few in Nazareth who had a little wealth and their sons were coveted.

Conversations of the coming Messiah brought talk of royalty and rule, of feasts and finery. I could not imagine what God's plan could be. It was as though he had taken every expectation and argument that man could devise and turned it on its head. Sending the Messiah through the poorest, the most insignificant, the unschooled, the unknown. It was incomprehensible. If I thought about it too long I found myself questioning over and over again. Surely I was the least qualified for such a task as this; fearful, selfish and so young. Could this child really be raised by a carpenter? One who had proved already incapable of protecting a child, one broken in pain and marred by loss? Both of us marked by failure. How could God use us?

"Mary," Joseph said, shaking my arm. "Mary, you must listen to me carefully."

The joy that I had just experienced with Elizabeth ebbed as the flow of difficulty and impossibility rose once again, reminding me of my inability to remain constant. The seriousness of his tone cut through my thoughts and I gave him my full attention.

"Mary, do you know what is happening?" asked Joseph.

I shook my head. My mind wondered back over the last week and I shuddered at the horror of it all. It was a powerless feeling to realize that life as I had known it no longer existed, and I felt as though the future was out of my hands.

"The Lord has kept you, He is watching over you," he explained.

"I don't understand, Joseph. Why did you come back to me?"

Even though he was here right now, the sting of abandonment was still raw.

"Mary, when you first told me about the child, I was
livid. I thought that you had betrayed me; the pain of it cut
more deeply than you can ever know. I was content to never
be with another woman after my wife…."

I reacted and pulled my hand out of his. I did not want
to compete with her memory. Joseph rose and circled the
room, hands joined behind his back but shoulders slumped.
I studied him wearily.

"I lost my wife many years ago and I never thought that
I would love again."

He turned and made his way back, taking my hand as
he took his seat beside me. Eyes downcast, I fought for the
moment, I fought to trust.

"My heart opened to you, Mary. My heart softened and
love found its way deep into my soul. It took time for me
to accept the opportunity but the Lord reassured me. I saw
that you were honorable and devoted to the scriptures. You
serve others with passion and are mature beyond your years.
I fasted many days until I knew that I was to take you as
my wife. I chose you, Mary. For better or worse, I made the
choice."

The words from our betrothal so many months before
echoed through my mind.

"The only justifiable course of action was to place all
the blame for the pregnancy on you, but you would have
paid for it with your life. The only other way was to divorce
you quietly and I was going to do it; retribution was mine
for the taking. Your family would have been dishonored
and you and the child would have been shamed for life but
a quiet divorce would have saved your life and spared my

reputation."

The birds chirped outside and the sweet scent of frangipane wafted through the window in stark contrast to the gravity of our conversation.

"It was many weeks," he went on. "My course was clear but I could not act as the weight of what you had done bore down on my heart. One night, I was startled by a presence in my room. I could not look directly at it as I could only make out the dancing swirls and shifting shapes of many beams of light. I looked to the side and then, out of the corner of my eye I could make out forms and structure. I had not experienced such strength, such power. The fragrance was intoxicating and sounds of heaven accompanied it; such colors, vivid and alive. I did not want to move in case it left or in case I was imagining it. The presence was awesome and I could tell that he came to me directly from God. I knew this had to be an angel.

'Joseph, son of David,' the being spoke. Its voice sounded unlike any human and echoed through generations. *'Do not be afraid to take Mary home as your wife, because what is conceived in her is from the Holy Spirit.*[17] *'*

"Tears poured from my eyes," he was clearly moved at the memory. "I had been so sure that I had made a mistake, that I had opened myself to love again, only to be wounded more deeply than ever before. The angel's words affirmed that I had chosen well but that God had chosen you also. I was deeply humbled."

He shifted so that we faced each other.

"Mary, the angel told me that we will have a son named Jesus," his voice lowered to a whisper and the room was thick with emotion. *'He will save his people from their sins.*[18] *'*

I closed my eyes as the truth of his words settled in my

heart and confirmed everything that had happened and that had been spoken to me. The loneliness subsided as I realized that that I would not be alone to carry this burden. I could barely take in what it all meant; the implications were indescribable.

"I wasted no time and returned to Nazareth as quickly as I could. I was on my way to see your abba when I heard the jeers of a crowd by the well. I felt an urgency and hurried towards the people when I would normally have avoided them. As I neared the crowd, I heard them cry out to stone you. My soul was on fire. I ran with the wind of heaven at my feet. My love for you and passion for this baby drove me through the mob that called for blood. I didn't care. I only thought of you, of the child."

He squeezed my hand, pausing momentarily. There was so much I wanted to say, more that I wanted to ask but I didn't want to disrespect him. He was already sharing more intimately than I could have hoped. I waited quietly, hoping that he would continue. He turned his gaze to the clay vessels in the corner but his focus was far in the distance. His hand moved habitually to his chin as he rubbed his beard.

Elizabeth made her way over and served our meal in silence. Zechariah entered and ate with us. I did not want to be left alone with them in this strange place. I had never been away from home before by myself. Even with my parents, my experiences outside of Nazareth were limited. Apprehension crawled over my skin as I knew that Joseph would soon be leaving. The unknown loomed before me. Bowls were gathered and Joseph began to rise to make final preparations. I grabbed his tunic, up on my knees now.

"Please, Joseph, don't leave yet," I sobbed.

He released his clothing from my hands and looked at

Elizabeth for help. She came and placed her hands gently on my shoulders.

"Mary, we are here for you. You will not be alone."

I shook off her embrace and took Joseph's hand again in desperation.

"Please, Joseph, there's one more thing," I pleaded desperately.

"What, Mary? What is troubling you?" he asked tenderly. He nodded at Elizabeth and I was thankful that she made her way back to the grinding stone.

"The other night," I tried to whisper but I could not hide the bitterness in my voice. "I heard Savta. I heard you all talking about the baby, about getting rid of it."

I pulled in breath and held it to stop the flow of tears that threatened to spill again. His own eyes filled. I waited for him to speak.

"There are those who are driven by fear, Mary," he finally said. "Your savta, she doesn't understand what is at stake. She is thinking only of you, of your family."

His words were strong and yet I was surprised at the compassion in them. He was not angry with Savta, only deeply sad. I sat down and wrapped my arms around my knees. I heard Elizabeth stir from the back of the room and felt awkward that she would overhear our conversation. Joseph paced.

I did not move despite the activity that now circled around me. I closed my eyes and let Joseph's words repeat in my head. I did not dare to tell him, to confess that I was no better than Savta. For a brief moment, she had offered me a way out of this. The anger that had risen up was not only towards her, it was towards myself. All I had wanted was for everything to go back to the way it was. I was no better than any of them and I hung my head in shame.

Twelve

Joseph appeared not to notice my silent retreat and our conversation ended. He went instead to make final preparations for his journey. He spoke briefly with Elizabeth leaving instructions for my safety. I did not move. Tears stung my eyes and dripped onto my clothes, shielded by the veil of hair that hung and hid. As he turned to leave, he placed his hand on my head and spoke a blessing over me and the baby, "May the Lord bless you and guard you."

His voice was gruff, strained. I wanted to cling to his hand, to hold it to my face and weep into the roughness; the comfort of calluses and dirt from years of heavy labor etched into his skin. These were the hands of a man who was not afraid of hard work; a man who had chosen a path that few would tread. I knew that I did not deserve him. I balled my fists in my lap so as not to expose my weakness. As he made his way to the door, bag slung over shoulder, I lifted my gaze and peered through my hair. Out of the corner of my eye I saw Elizabeth watching me, watching him. I was embarrassed. What had she seen? What did she think of me? The intensity of the moment passed as Joseph left. I rose quickly and turned away, stumbling to the back of the house where I could leave through the stable without Joseph seeing. I needed some time, some escape.

"Where are you going, child?" asked Elizabeth anxiously. "You cannot leave."

"Who says?" I asked aggressively. It was uncharacteristic and yet I was driven to relieve the tension inside.

"You heard Joseph just now," her voice softened. "Please Mary, we just want to care for you. No one here wants to hurt you but you are not in Nazareth anymore. These streets are not safe for a woman alone and you might get lost."

She paused; I wilted slightly.

"If you like, we can walk together. I will accompany you to the well perhaps. Some fresh air would do us both some good."

She stood, wiping her hand. I did not want to go with her. I wanted to be alone but my resolve had dissipated. I shook my head and slouched to my mattress without a word, weeping into my arms until sleep finally overtook.

I awoke as afternoon slipped into dusk. Hair matted and stuck to my face. My anguish sent waves of stinging, throbbing pain across my chest and down my arms. I groaned and rolled over. Tears leaked and burned my cheeks, although sobs were finally exhausted. I had to focus on every breath but secretly wished that I could just stop. Just stop breathing and fall asleep and make it all stop.

Elizabeth broke my thoughts as she entered the house with a basket of olives. She was singing to herself; a joyful melody that filled the room, and I realized that she was still laughing. How could she be so happy, so inconsiderate? Had Joseph not told her what had happened to me? Had she not seen me run to my bed this morning? I felt ignored, disregarded, and wondered why he had brought me here. I stayed in bed as long as I could until the aches of pregnancy forced me to rise. I skirted the room and then sat with my back to Elizabeth. A trail of ants caught my attention and I let my focus rest on them. Elizabeth said nothing but prepared the press to receive oil from the olives. I was becoming thirsty and faint with hunger but still she said nothing. The nausea from the pregnancy was getting worse and I was dizzy with sickness.

"I need water," I whispered, my voice dry and cracked.

"Of course," Elizabeth sang, the words were wrapped in joy and I could not look at her. "You can have anything you want. This is your home now."

She brought a cup of water and I drank it greedily. Thoughts of home filled my mind, bringing with them a new degree of darkness. Abba, Ima, what were they doing? Did they care about me now? Savta, did she love me anymore? I leaned against the coolness of the wall.

"You must eat, Mary," Elizabeth crooned.

She put a plate of bread and figs in front of me but I could not eat even though my stomach growled in anticipation. It was another hour before I opened my eyes again. Zechariah came through the door. What an odd man, small framed and skinny but hardly able to coordinate his movements or keep control of his limbs. His legs seemed to go in opposite directions and his arms danced constantly. He removed his shoes and sat so that Elizabeth could wash his feet. He kept tapping her on the head or shoulders to get her attention and then waving his arms and hands wildly. She nodded and answered with understanding. I could not help but stare. When he finally looked in my direction, I caught his eye before quickly putting my head against the wall and closing my eyes again. His face was strong and did not fit his scrawny body. His jaw and brow were wide and his cheekbones rose high above his beard making him almost beautiful. His eyes were black, large and round and appeared to see right into my soul. At first he unnerved me but then curiosity got the better of me. I opened my eyes again and gave a shout, falling backwards. He was sitting silently, cross-legged in front of me, staring. He took my arm and pulled me back to my seat. Taking the bread and pressing it into my hand, he motioned for me to eat. I shook my head and looked away. Still holding the bread in my hand he took his other hand and moved my face to look at him. He motioned again for me to eat and then pointed at my belly. I felt self-conscious and shook my head again. He threw my hand down and gestured wildly at Elizabeth.

"Hamuda," she said, "you must eat. If you can't eat for yourself, you must do it for your child."

Zechariah picked up the bread again and lifted my hand to my face so that I could take a bite. The smell of the bread encouraged me and as I ate, the sweetness of Elizabeth's endearment also filled my soul. 'Hamuda; dear one'. The food energized and lifted my spirits. I ate slowly and Zechariah left. Candles flickered on the walls casting shadows over rugs and furniture. The sounds of the city, so unfamiliar, still roared outside despite the late hour.

"Who is he?" I asked.

"Zechariah?" Elizabeth asked. "Why, he is my husband." She paused, her eyes filled with admiration. "He is much respected."

She smiled broadly and giggled, then laughed loudly, unable to regain her composure for several minutes. My eyes widened and I didn't know what to do or say. Zechariah ran into the house, his mouth opening and closing as though he was trying to say something. He kept pointing at Elizabeth and jumping up and down, pointing outside, his arms swinging in circles above his head.

"I know, I know," Elizabeth gulped.

"I can't help it. The neighbors will just have to talk."

Zechariah threw up his hands and stormed out of the house. Elizabeth sat down and after several minutes was able to talk again.

"He is a good and wise man; my behavior upsets him and the neighbors are mocking me. Zechariah is a priest, an honorable man in the sight of God. He has served blamelessly, observing all the Lord's commandments and regulations."

She tried to stifle more laughter but was completely overcome once again. I was frustrated. This strange behavior made me uncomfortable. I went back to my bed and slept deeply until morning.

I awoke with the cockerel and sat up, wondering where I was. Dawn broke rosy with the lure of a new day and beckoned me. I stood by the window and watched the soft glow of dawn give way to the oppressive reality of the blazing sun. I wanted to go home. My life was in tatters and here I was in hiding with a drunkard and a mute. It added to my humiliation. I felt trapped. Trapped by the baby in my womb, trapped by fear of death, trapped once again by hopelessness. I spent the next two weeks in a haze of tears and self-pity. I ate whatever Elizabeth put in front of me but I never asked for food. I slept when the sun set and rose only when hunger forced. I sat on the roof late in each afternoon to avoid the heat of the sun and the looks from the women passing below as they fetched water and gossiped. Thankfully, I was able to keep out of sight and Elizabeth drew all attention and speculation away from me. Perhaps people didn't even know I was there but I felt exposed and it was easier to stay out of the way.

Zechariah's silence and my refusal to talk meant that the only sound in the house was Elizabeth's laughter. For two weeks it hadn't subsided. The sound of it became familiar and that's when it stopped.

Thirteen

"Hamuda, it is time for us to talk," Elizabeth spoke somberly while we ate breakfast. I had not seen her this way; calm, sad even. I was intrigued. She waited for a response but I gave none.

"Your heart is downcast. I have sought the Lord and asked Him why your soul is so disturbed. I have no answers for you child, but I have a story. Perhaps it will bring you hope."

I was thankful that she did not try to talk me out of my despair. I hadn't realized how closely she empathized and her compassion stirred me to listen.

"I am an old woman," she began. "Perhaps I am like

Sarah although I would not dare to say that I am a woman of her faith and stature. For many years I have longed for a child. Since I was small, I have dreamed of being a mother but I was unable to carry a child. I conceived once in my earlier years but I lost the child almost as soon as I discovered that I was pregnant. The pain scarred my heart and I have been unable to be freed from grief. My only comfort was in serving the Lord. Once I realized that He was not to blame and even that I was not to blame, I found peace. I could not explain why such a thing would happen and so I did not try. I don't know how I would have survived otherwise; year after year watching my friends and neighbors birthing child after child, attending circumcisions, *bar mitzvahs*, watching the children play by the well. Not to mention the scorn I endured; whispers silenced as I approached, overheard conversations, rejection and speculation of my sin or what curse had inflicted this shame upon me. A woman can never escape its grip.

"One day, as I was kneading the bread, I looked down at my hands and saw the veins bulging, or perhaps it was just that my hands were withering. Frail and speckled with age, I began to realize that my time was coming to an end on this earth. I thanked God for the many years that He had given me. I had no regrets and smiled as memories filed through my mind; I spoke a brief prayer as I committed my life and spirit into His hands. All of a sudden pain gripped my heart. I wondered if He had taken me at my word but I did not die. My hands reached instinctively to my heart in some vain way to alleviate the pressure. It was then that I remembered the words of the psalmist: *He heals the broken-hearted and binds up their wounds.*[19] Suddenly the pain left and I heard in my spirit, 'It's not over yet.'

"I returned to my kneading, wondering what had just happened and what those words meant. Three days later, Zechariah was preparing to be on duty at the temple in Jerusalem. He was chosen by lot to go into the Holy Place and burn incense. Many worshippers were assembled and praying outside. I was among them but stayed towards the back. It was a great honor for a priest to enter the temple and I didn't want to draw any attention to myself. Zechariah was inside much longer than was customary and the people began to get agitated. I had already returned home as the crowd was rowdy and I didn't understand what was taking so long. I left before they could direct their questions at me. When he finally came out, he was as white as a sheet and could not talk. The people accused him of witchcraft but he kept making signs to them until they realized that he had seen a vision. Zechariah stayed at the temple to finish his time of service and then returned home several days later. I did not press him to tell me what had happened. The first few days he was coming to terms with the silence and spent much time in prayer. I could see that he was very frustrated and so I left him to find his peace.

"Some time later, an extraordinary thing happened. You must remember I was barren and also much past the age of menstruation. I had been sick for some weeks but it always passed before lunch. It had been five months since Zechariah's encounter in the temple. I finally expressed to him my concern over the sickness, and also that I had become very light headed. I had found a hard lump in my abdomen and I was afraid that I was stricken with tumors. Zechariah began to jump up and down. He ran to the tablet that he had bought so that he could write to me as it was the only way we could communicate when I couldn't understand his hand gestures. He wrote, 'baby' and then pointed at my belly. I shook my head.

" 'That's not possible,' I responded skeptically.

"For the first time, he recounted the details of that day at the temple. The vision of the angel, how he had questioned the angel's message and had been struck silent. He had not wanted to share the message with me in case it did not come true."

"Mary," she looked at me and took my hand. "God has made the impossible possible. He has taken what was dried up and near death and infused me with new life. The angel told my husband that our son will do great things but the greatest of these will be to prepare the way for the Lord."

Her tender eyes filled with tears.

"Joseph visited us and stayed for several weeks as soon as he found out that you were pregnant. He had heard my brother, Joachim speak highly of Zechariah and he turned to him for help and counsel. We were both deeply shocked. I, like many others, was filled with disgust and shame; I have been raised to follow the law and to be devoted to the Torah. Such a confession was a travesty and we watched for many days as Joseph wrestled with God. My husband carried a heavy burden of prayer. He knew that Joseph's load was great and yet only God could provide a way through. Joseph and Zechariah sat for many hours together as Joseph poured out his fears and pain but Zechariah was unable to respond. Sometimes his heart almost burst and yet he could offer little more than a hand on the shoulder. This went on for a long time as Joseph seemed to traverse the darkest of valleys. Finally, one day he emerged. He had passed through I suppose. He sat down with both Zechariah and I and asked if you could stay with us until he was ready to take you as his wife. He feared that your life was in danger. I had not responded in the same way as my husband and I scorned Joseph for not divorcing you. To me, that was the way of justice. My own heart ached for his pain and I did not want you in my home. All I saw was your sin, but my husband is a compassionate man. He took his tablet and wrote, 'Joseph is a righteous man and we will do as he asked.' I was not prepared to receive you well. I was afraid of what the neighbors would say. I was ashamed to go to the temple. I had resolved to keep you out of sight and to speak very little to you.

"When you and Joseph arrived at our home, I was filled with anger. Zechariah warned me to be silent and instructed me to prepare food as you would be hungry. He ran out to greet you as best he could. I came to the door and forced my welcome but at the sound of your voice, I was completely overcome with joy. For two weeks I could hardly talk. I had little to give to you, Mary. There was nothing that I could say or even wanted to say, but I watched you. I watched you weep, I watched your shame, I watched the darkness hover over you and slowly my heart was changed and I was filled with compassion.

"One day as I was baking, I prayed for you. It was the first time. I asked God to take away your shame, and then I was reminded of a word that my savta spoke to me when I was a child. Any time I did anything wrong, she would say, 'Hamuda, dear one, come to me.' I would crawl on her lap and she would stroke my hair. My father would come to punish we with the switch but Savta said, 'Not now, her heart must first be touched by love.'

She reached for my hand.

" 'Mary,' she spoke. 'Hamuda, you have done nothing

wrong. The child in your womb has come to replace fear with love, and to bring comfort instead of the rod.' "

I felt the pressure ease at her words. Here I was loved and accepted. For the first time I felt vindicated, if only slightly. Perhaps the whole world was against me but I had found an advocate. I found great comfort with Elizabeth after our conversation. Indeed, the impossible had been made possible. The days ahead loomed large and yet my fear was relegated to the unknown rather than to the abandonment and punishment that I had previously felt.

My days were punctuated with moments of great faith and then the lack thereof. It was Elizabeth's wisdom that changed my course and pointed me in the right direction. She seemed to anticipate my mood and even my thoughts at times.

"Hamuda," she said gently but with a strength that grabbed my attention. "You must stop looking around you and look only to the face of our God. Let go of yesterday and take hold of His hand; trade tomorrow for His promises."

Slowly, day-by-day, my confidence grew. My inadequacy was being replaced with the knowledge of His competence. My unworthiness was transformed as my belly swelled with royalty. As I silenced my beating heart and sat desperately in His presence, my fears were plucked and love poured in and over. I realized that even my name reflected the choice before me. Would I be Mary, the bitter, or Miriam, the mirror of God? Both names had been assigned to me and yet who would I be? The idea of reflecting God seemed arrogant and proud and yet His very self dwelt inside me, attached. Our heartbeats were one. His blood coursed through mine and mine in his. This reality broke the back of everything

I had known before. A new reality was being carved out in my life. At times it was too much to comprehend but then, when his goodness overshadowed, I was gripped by a new principle. This God who I had served with devotion had approached me, not as a servant, but as a trusted one, as one who would learn to love. My days grew in this new understanding. I began to trust the hand of God, instead of being consumed by the work of man. Even though my circumstances had not changed, something inside me had. I was still faced with the daily choice to trust, but a divine reality had been established.

I helped Elizabeth bake bread and press the olives and also to prepare the house for her baby. We sewed garments for both of our boys and laughed together as we pictured them together playing. As the time neared for Elizabeth to give birth, she became increasingly tired and I took on most of the household tasks while she rested. I was thankful to be able to serve when she needed help the most. I could see that she was anxious about the birth but I had no way to reassure her. Perhaps it is better to not know what is coming. I still don't know how she survived.

Fourteen

The contractions had been regular but weak for a month. They caused Elizabeth to catch her breath and lay down. Many times, Zechariah sent for the midwife but she confirmed each time that Elizabeth was not in labor. I wondered how she could even walk with such a load. She was a small woman and her belly had grown so that it hung low by her hips, supported by cloth tied around her body to give her back some relief. She bent under the strain and the kicks of her child were strong, relentless. He never gave a moment's peace and sleep came only in short spurts. She lay on her side panting for breath and pressing the child away from ribs and lungs; her belly rolled under his movements. My own was tiny in comparison. Still, I wondered how I could continue to expand without exploding. Elizabeth's ankles and face had swelled and I felt sorry for her, although I never heard her complain.

I woke up early one morning; it was past Elizabeth's ninth month. I heard her groaning and the midwife was there. I jumped out of bed and ran to take Elizabeth's hand. Zechariah was as white as a sheet, his silent lips praying.

"Help me," the midwife spoke gruffly. "Take her other arm and help me move her to the pallet."

Elizabeth lay down while we prepared the birthing stones around the hole in the ground in which to catch the baby. Pillows and cloths were laid out and the midwife arranged warm poultices and fomentations to alleviate the pain. All morning Elizabeth labored. The pains never came more frequently or increased in intensity, but neither did they give her any respite. By mid-afternoon she was already so exhausted that she slept between contractions, waking up with a groan as each tightening awoke her. I sat beside her constantly, pressing a wet rag to her lips and dripping honey into her mouth. Women came and went to attend her and assist the midwife. Zechariah stayed at the synagogue to pray. I would not leave Elizabeth's side and lay down next to her. I slept when she slept and I groaned when she groaned. She gripped my hand so hard at times that I thought she might break my fingers. By nightfall, there was still no sign of the baby. I asked the midwife why it was taking so long.

"Babies come in their own time, child," she replied.

I didn't like it that she called me child.

"Is there nothing you can do," I asked, my voice wavered with concern.

"Give her this." She shoved a cup into my hand. "Make

sure she drinks it all."

The stuff smelled foul and Elizabeth gagged when I poured it into her mouth. I spoke gently and encouraged her to drink. Soon after there was a gush of water and I looked hopefully at the women surrounding. They scurried, tripping over one another by candlelight, bringing rags and clean clothes. Elizabeth did not want to be moved or even touched. She was so tired, she could barely open her eyes.

"Prepare the pennyroyal," the midwife instructed one of the attending women. The tea seemed to ease the pain. The neighbors chatted amongst themselves while labor continued. For much of the process it seemed that there was little for them to do.

"Come child," said the midwife. "You must rest. The other women can sit with her."

I was reluctant to leave Elizabeth's side but I was exhausted. I wondered how she could do this, to be in pain for so long.

"I will call for you when it is time; for now you must sleep," urged the midwife more strongly. "I will need you when the time comes."

I relented, kissing Elizabeth's forehead. I prayed that she would survive. It took a while to fall asleep as my mind raced. The groaning from Elizabeth finally lulled me. They were coming more often since the gush of water and she seemed to have to draw from a deeper place within. Still, she did not move.

I don't know how long I slept. I had lost all track of time but I awoke in the darkest hour of the night, to someone shaking me awake.

"Get up, we need you," the voice said urgently.

As memories of the previous day broke through my

sleepiness, I hurried anxiously from bed. There was only one other woman with the midwife; the soft flicker of candlelight illuminated the sweat that seared Elizabeth's brow. I lit the lamps and the room filled with light and energy. Elizabeth had been laboring for close to 24 hours. Skin pale and clammy; hair drenched with sweat; her body shook uncontrollably and I rushed to her side.

"I'm here, Elizabeth," I whispered as I knelt beside her, leaning over her ear. She turned her face towards me but didn't open her eyes. "The Lord will strengthen you," I added. She smiled and took my hand. I fought the urge to cry.

"Come now," said Sarah, the other woman. "Help us get ready. It won't be long now."

Water boiled on the fire and we tidied the room in preparation although there was little to be done. I took soiled rags outside and breathed in the cool air to clear my head. My hands moved instinctively to my belly as the child inside me stirred. I hoped that I would have the strength to endure such an ordeal. Wailing from inside the house shattered my thoughts. I rushed back to Elizabeth's side.

"Help us lift her onto the stones," instructed the midwife.

It took all three of us to pull her off the pallet. Sarah and myself each took an arm over our shoulders. The midwife helped guide her feet onto the birthing stones. We lowered her down into a squatting position; head hung and knees shaking. The midwife checked her. I couldn't see what she was doing beyond the cloths draped over Elizabeth's legs. She looked relieved as she sat up and wiped her hands.

"The head is down," she uttered. "She is not quite ready though."

My heart sank. The midwife sat up on her knees and

leaned into Elizabeth, taking her hand.

"Your baby will be here soon but I must help get you ready. It will hurt." She returned to the floor and disappeared from sight again.

With the next contraction, Elizabeth threw back her head; hands grasping for something to hold and I put mine in hers. As the contraction passed, she panted; her small shoulders lifting and dropping with each breath.

"The bowl," she whispered, eyes opening frantically.

Sarah grabbed the bowl next to her and put it in front of Elizabeth. She had eaten so little but the urge to vomit was strong.

"Get her water," directed the midwife. "And more honey."

She took a sip of the water but turned her head away from the honey.

The midwife was still lying across the floor. "Did she take the honey?" she asked.

I muttered my response weakly, "No."

"What, child?" the midwife barked. "Speak up!" She looked at me beyond the cloths. "I have enough to take care of here without trying to cajole you. You might be a *betulah*, but today you grow up. Make her take the honey," she commanded.

I wished that I could leave. The midwife's tone was salt on a wound. Being a betulah was something to be proud of but she had scorned me. I turned my attention to Elizabeth and forced the spoon past her lips. I hoped that my silence would indicate that the midwife's reprimand had been ineffective, yet it stuck. The smell of honey brought a sweet recollection; honey breath and the overpowering strength of Heaven's love. I rested in the moment as time slowed.

Love grew; wound healed.

The contractions continued until the sun rose over the horizon. The soft rosy glow reminded me of lazy days following the harvest when our bodies still wanted to rise early but the day stretched endlessly ahead. Elizabeth cried out over and over. Between each contraction, we leaned her back on a stool to give us a rest from holding her up, and to take the pressure off her legs. When I thought I couldn't stand it one more time, the midwife sat up, wiping her brow and reaching for a cup of water. She drank the whole cup; face flushed with exertion, her eyes bloodshot and weary from the many hours of labor. There was little time before the next contraction. We hauled Elizabeth upright again.

"Whenever you are ready, push," the midwife instructed.

A sound like I had never heard before rose up out of Elizabeth. It started in the deepest parts of her being. Quiet, barely audible and then louder, louder as it rose up through her chest and out of her mouth. Her whole body stiffened, her hands clenched and she lifted her head, mouth open. She roared. I was surprised at the power of it. Just moments before she had hung limply in our arms and somehow she had transformed before our eyes as the delivery took over.

"Good, good," said the midwife. "Just a few more like that and you will be holding your child."

Elizabeth sobbed. The contractions came much quicker now and with each one she emitted the same sound. Many times over she cried out and even at times called for God to take away her suffering. Finally, as the sun rose high, the baby pushed his way into the world. The midwife caught him in a blanket and wiped him. He let out a hearty cry and Elizabeth leaned forward to see her son.

"Wait!" shouted the midwife. "Sit her back," she

instructed.

I could barely move, my muscles seized, bones stiff from being in the same position for so long. I bit my lip so that I didn't make a sound. We lowered Elizabeth back onto the stool. She leaned her head against my shoulder and I wiped a wet rag over her forehead.

"You did it, Elizabeth," I whispered. "You have your son."

Elizabeth laughed and sobbed at the same time.

"Is it really over?" she moaned, looking pathetically into my eyes.

I looked at the midwife who was still busy with the baby.

As I looked down I cried out, falling backwards and almost taking Elizabeth with me. Thankfully, Sarah was still holding onto her. The midwife shot me an indignant look.

"What is wrong with you?" she hissed.

The baby was shocking; skin waxy, head squeezed. Blood poured from Elizabeth. I felt like I was going to faint.

"Get out of here," the midwife hissed again. "Get out!"

Fifteen

I crawled out of the house as quickly as I could. I saw the look of panic on Elizabeth's face as I hurried out of the door. The midwife put a hand on her knee.

"He's perfect," she reassured.

I moved out of the street to the side of the house where only the mid-morning sun reached. I splashed water on my face from the rain barrel and sank to the ground to rest. The water ran streaks down dirt-laden cheeks but could not cleanse me of the images. The violence of it left me shuddering. I had always heard of the miracle of birth but what I had just seen was brutal, cruel. What would I have to go through to bring this child into the world; a world fraught with danger and a life already marked by death? How could something so ugly ever be called perfect? I wanted to escape but I had nowhere to go. Head buried in hands, I wept. I dared not make a sound but my whole body convulsed with sobs. Sleep finally carried me away and I woke while the sun was high. Zechariah stood aloft, prodding my shoulder and pushing the hair away from my face with a stick. Legs stuck straight out in front; my head had fallen awkwardly to the side sending spasms shooting down my neck when I tried to move, face hot and burned from the sun. He helped me sit upright and I shook off further attempts of help. He was pointing madly at the house and rocking his arms. Hair and eyes wild, he looked as though he hadn't slept since the labor started.

Elizabeth! I pulled my knees under me and managed to haul myself to standing but the ground lurched and sky spun. Zechariah grabbed my elbows as I crashed back to the ground. Blood seeped from a gash on my forehead, mingling with the sweat and grime of the last two days. One of Elizabeth's neighbors came running and pressed a rag to my head to stop the bleeding. Before I knew what was happening, I was being half carried, half dragged to her house where I slept until nightfall. I awoke to the sounds of children playing around me. The woman who had come to my aid knelt beside me.

"Don't try to move," she spoke kindly. "Do you feel like you could eat?"

I nodded eagerly. She fetched a bowl of lamb broth and propped my head on a pillow so she could feed me. I kept my eyes closed but listened while she spoke.

"Elizabeth is fine and her baby is strong," her voice was gentle and soothing.

"He's a big boy though, it's no wonder he gave her so much trouble. I heard the midwife just about gave up on them both."

She reprimanded one of the children around her and continued to feed me in silence. I stayed for two days, and slept for most of it before I was able to return to Elizabeth's house.

I walked anxiously across the street, my footsteps leaving no imprint on the dry, cracked ground. The path veered to the left and dropped at a slight incline past houses that were almost stacked one on top of the other, they were so close. Zechariah and Elizabeth's house was set back from the others, hidden. The door was closed and I wasn't sure if I should knock. Zechariah saw me from the hill behind the house and came running and waving his hands, leaping adeptly over rocks, dodging boulders and trees that stood randomly in his way. He took my hand as he approached and shook it up and down. I think he would have hugged me, eyes gleaming. I smiled warmly and asked if I could go in. He nodded and led me through the door. Elizabeth sat across the room on a pile of blankets, her little bundle cradled in arms while she sang to him.

"Hamuda, I have been so worried about you," she said. "Come and see."

I was astounded at her resilience. Was it possible that she had been so close to death just two days ago?

"Come and sit with us," she said, patting the empty space on the blanket beside her.

I lowered myself carefully onto the blanket, hardly daring to breathe. I braced myself as she turned the baby so that I could see his face. His beauty took my breath away. The violence of birth had been replaced by the angel softness of new life. Locks of dark hair curled around his ears and forehead. His cheeks were round and pink with the exertion of nursing; lips puckered and perfect. How he ever fit inside Elizabeth I could not imagine. She pulled the swaddling cloths aside to reveal limbs that rolled with chubby fat and I looked in awe.

"The Lord has done this for me," she whispered, unable to take her eyes off the child. *"He has shown his favor and taken away my disgrace among the people.*[20]*"*

For the next week, I cooked and took care of the house so that Elizabeth could rest and care for the child. Nursing was very difficult and she wept bitterly each time he turned his little face, searching for milk. When it was over, the agony was swept quickly away as kisses erased the memory. Whenever I could, I sat beside her, our closeness bringing comfort. I spoke little. Sometimes, she would lay the child on the blanket beside her and wrap me in her arms instead.

On the eighth day after the birth, we were preparing for the circumcision. I was sweeping the floor and brushing the dust and dirt out of the front door when I was startled by a familiar voice.

"Mary!"

I turned apprehensively in case it was my imagination. Dropping the broom, I cried out.

"Abba! Ima!"

I leapt into their arms, never wanting to let go until Abba whispered in my ear, "Joseph traveled with us, Mary. He is here also."

I turned, heart pounding. Was I dreaming? *I looked for the one my heart loves*[21]. I lifted my hand to my eyes, straining to see down the hill and then I saw him, *coming up from the desert, like a column of smoke*[22]. I waited until he reached me.

He did not take my hand or touch me but he looked long, searching my eyes.

"How beautiful you are, my darling,[23]*"* he whispered so that only I could hear him.

I hardly dared breathe, fearing that I would betray unchecked passion. My parents guided us into the house where there was great rejoicing over the birth of the child. Ima squealed at the sight of Elizabeth holding the baby.

"Elizabeth! How I have missed you! And to think that you have received what you have longed for after all these years," Ima stooped to kiss Elizabeth, tears pouring over the child who grunted and squirmed in his mother's arms.

Abba and Zechariah stood shaking each other's hands. Pride burst out of Zechariah as Abba congratulated him over and over. Joseph smiled peacefully at the scene as I tucked in beside him, breathing deep the pungent scent of earthy linen and days of travel. The house became a frenzy of activity as we ate and talked, one over the other. Preparations were quickly made for the ceremony that would take place early that same evening. Ima baked and prepared the food while I finished cleaning and decorating the house with the color and fragrance of purple iris, poppies, yellow tulips and pink carnations.

The little house was soon filled with neighbors, and the *mohel* came to perform the circumcision. Food was carried in and affection bestowed on the sleeping baby's head. Elizabeth sat serenely as years of anguish and months of speculation evaporated in joy and celebration. The room slowly fell to a hush as the mohel began the *brit milah* with his profound, lyrical recitation of the Torah. I wept, closing my eyes and swaying in the heat of the room. I pictured my ancestors, the mothers. I wondered about the women of the

Exodus, giving birth and raising children in captivity and then in exile; of Sarah who reminded me of Elizabeth; of Hannah who had also suffered in barrenness. What had Sarah gone through when she realized that Abraham had taken Isaac to be sacrificed? I shuddered. These stories that I had loved my whole life suddenly became alive as I connected emotionally, perhaps for the first time. I pushed my way to the back of the crowded room and gasped for evening's cool air. I turned the corner to the side of the house and fell to my knees. Knuckles bleached white; clasped hands thrown over bowed head, I cried out to God.

"Why, God? Why me? You know my weakness. Why did you choose me? Please God, I can't do this, I can't do this."

My throat squeezed; it became hard to breathe. My head dropped further still and I gripped my hands over my mouth.

"Please, do something. I can't do this," whispered agony. "I can't do what Elizabeth just did. I'm not strong like the women of the Torah. I'm not like them. Please, please …."

Hands fell gently but firmly on my shoulders. I felt the strong embrace of love around me and I leaned my head back as tears rolled down my face. The smell of my beloved was intoxicating; the feel of his arms on mine brought comfort. He rested his chin on my head so that I felt covered, safe. Fear melted in love's presence.

Suddenly I heard Ima's voice.

"Mary, are you alright?" she asked.

I scrambled to my feet, disoriented and embarrassed that she had seen me like this in Joseph's arms but as I quickly turned, he was nowhere to be found.

"Mary, what is it?" Ima pressed.

"Joseph, he was just here," I answered, unable to look

her in the eye.

"No, Mary. Joseph is in the house assisting the mohel. No one else is out here."

Sixteen

Confusion crossed my face. The sound of singing drifted out of the house and mingled with the warm breeze of evening.

"Mary, come and sit. I will get you a drink." She ushered me to a bench and disappeared inside; Heaven's whisper echoed.

I looked at Ima and, as she sat beside me, tears trickled. She grasped my face in her hands as our tears fell together over aged fingers. She smelled of soap and baking.

I watched her face, weary and drawn with the strain of the last months but it was her heart that concerned me as I saw the wounds it bore.

"I'm sorry," I whispered. "I never would have put you through all of this."

She sat beside me, calm, collected, as she patted my hand affectionately. We looked out over the valley towards Jerusalem.

"We receive grace for what we must endure," she spoke peacefully. "Who of us would have chosen the path our feet travel if we could have seen what lay ahead? And yet we press onward, our hope fixed on Him. He sees it all from the beginning to the end. We cannot stop in the middle of our journey to doubt, or rage, or shake a fist, for we do not know what is around the next corner. Every dark night beckons the most brilliant dawn. My own journey has brought me to my knees at times, and sometimes to my face, but it is in those moments that I feel Him lift my head and carry me. Would I trade the path for an easier one, for one that I could walk alone in comfort? Many do. Compromise and complacency is the enemy of a life truly lived. I would rather face the giant with God on my side than to slink in the shadows of self-preservation. You must not be sorry, Mary. God is rising up and we are part of His story. We do not see the end but we are confident; confident in Him for no matter the cost, no matter the pain, it all comes down to this one thing."

She placed a hand on my belly. The child stilled in my womb and we were caught up in the essence of our collective journeys. For a moment it felt as though the whole world held its breath; as though all of history had fought in existence and purpose for this moment, and that the future hinged on this child. The earth released its breath as the frivolity of celebration called us back. I made my way into the house and found a stool in the corner where I sat contemplating what had happened. Perhaps I would never know why I had been chosen. Perhaps I would never feel worthy or adequate for this task, but who was I to judge God? The celebration lasted well into the night. Exhausted, I crept to my bed and fell asleep quickly despite the shouts and songs that filled the house

The sound of silence startled me awake the next morning. I got up quickly feeling refreshed and strangely hopeful. The house was still decked with garlands and flowers drooping, shedding petals. I stoked the fire and collected water quietly, then swept the floor coated with dust and food, ushering a stray mouse outside as I made my way around the room. Zechariah and Elizabeth slept soundly on their pallets; Ima still curled up on the mattress next to mine. I heard Abba's rhythmic snoring from the roof. I began the preparations for breakfast and the smell of hot food caused everyone to stir and make their way into the room.

"Good morning, Mary. This is a day of celebration!" shouted Zechariah as he lifted his son from Elizabeth's arms. He held him high above his head before bringing him close to his chest and dancing around in circles, never once taking his eyes off the babe.

Everyone laughed as my eyes grew large, mouth open. I followed his movements, unable to take my eyes off him.

"It's alright, Mary," Elizabeth laughed. "You missed the best part of the celebration! Oh, I wish you had seen everyone's faces."

Abba came and sat beside me, taking my hand.

"Don't be afraid, Mary," he spoke softly. "Our God who has shown himself mighty to our ancestors, is doing miracles among us. Can you believe it, Mary? Who are we but peasants? Ha! The presence of the Lord came to this house last night and opened Zechariah's mouth."

"Abba," I looked at him for answers. "I don't understand."

He explained the events of the previous night in great detail, reliving the joy in each description. Abba was an avid storyteller, reenacting each character's position and recreating the scene entirely.

"The mohel arrived," he began, hurrying to the door and entering the room with a stately gait, eyes lifted piously to heaven. He relaxed, laughed and went on, moving quickly to the center of the room and turning, arms wide to portray the crowds of people.

"Everyone was calling the baby 'Zechariah.' " Arms lifted, eyes wide. He pointed to Elizabeth's pillow where the baby lay.

"Elizabeth kept trying to speak but her words were drowned by many voices." Arms pumped up and down. "As the proceedings began, the room fell silent. Zechariah and Elizabeth leapt from their seats together causing quite a commotion."

" *'No! He is to be called John,*[24]' your aunt repeated over and over. The room buzzed with murmured objections. 'It's unheard of,' spoke a neighbor. 'The first born son is always named after his father. *There's no one among your relatives who has that name*[25]. He must be Zechariah.' "

Abba pushed out his belly to imitate the neighbor, and deepened his voice, we all laughed at the mimic. He went on.

"A wave of agreement swept through the room." He spun around, knees bent, arm stretched out, his voice low, somber now. "So vital are our traditions and laws that to disrupt them or reject them is seen as defiance." He stood to attention, arm raised above his head. "Loyalty is closely guarded and any threat to our cohesion is not well tolerated."

"What next, Abba?" I asked, as he had paused for a moment too long. He turned and looked at me.

"The ruckus in the room escalated until Zechariah reached for his shepherd's hook."

Abba ran to the wall to fetch the hook, now imitating Zechariah.

"He beat it on the ground, sending clouds of dust into the air until the room calmed down."

We all started to cough as Abba filled the room with a cloud.

"He motioned for Elizabeth to get his writing tablet," Abba continued, "while the men around him made signs asking him what he would like to name the child. The room held its breath and all eyes watched in astonishment as he formed each letter. *His name is John.[26]*' Just as the room was about to fall into chaos, Zechariah's mouth was opened; tongue loosed so that he could speak.

" 'His name is John! His name is John! His name is John!' Zechariah bellowed the words allowing nine months of silence to escape in triumph."

Abba laughed and stomped his feet, waving his hands in the air.

" 'Look what God has done!' Zechariah declared. 'I have a son! My wife was dried up and now life has poured out of her as though she were a young girl.' "

Abba stomped and danced around the room, swinging the hook above his head, continuing his reenactment.

"As praises filled his mouth, he began to prophecy over the child, declaring, *Blessed be the Lord, the God of Israel; he came and set his people free. He set the power of salvation in the center of our lives, and in the very house of David his servant, just as he promised long ago through the preaching of his holy prophets: deliverance from our enemies and every hateful hand; mercy to our fathers, as he remembers to do what he said he'd do, what he swore to our father Abraham — a clean rescue from the enemy camp. So we can worship him without a care in the world, made holy before him as long as we live.*

And you, my child, "Prophet of the Highest," will go ahead of the Master to prepare his ways, present the offer of salvation to his people, the forgiveness of their sins. Through the heartfelt mercies of our God, God's Sunrise will break in upon us, shining on those in the darkness, those sitting in the shadow of death, then showing us the way, one foot at a time, down the path of peace.[27] ' "

Abba slumped down onto a stool, gasping for breath, weeping at the recollection.

"His whoops and hollers continued until everyone in the room could not help but join him. The ground shook as men leapt into the air, embracing Zechariah and hitting each other on the back.

" *'What is this child going to be?*[28] ' they called out to each other."

Everyone laughed at my face, jaw hanging open.

"Come, Mary, feed us our breakfast," ordered Zechariah, his eyes glinting with humor.

I was surprised at the depth and strength of his voice, a stark contrast to his stature. We all came to our senses and sat to eat. All that I had heard, as well as what I had experienced the night before overwhelmed and I sat quietly, taking it all in.

Joseph arrived at lunchtime. I waited for him to approach while he greeted my father and Zechariah. I glanced sideways at Ima who glowed with understanding. I knew that she approved of Joseph and here, away from Nazareth, she was free to enjoy unreservedly. Joseph sat opposite me, beside Abba. I felt his attention and smiled warmly when our eyes met. His beard was thick, skin darker than I remembered. We ate lightheartedly, the baby sucking on his fist on a blanket where we could all admire him. As Ima gathered the leftovers and plates, Abba spoke.

"It has been decided that Joseph and Mary must wed immediately. The elders of Nazareth have agreed that a small, private ceremony at Elizabeth's house will suffice. There are to be no witnesses other than those of us in this room today. Their terms are such that there must be no talk of this child being of God and you must return to Nazareth married and never speak of the wedding so that all the events of the last months can be forgotten. The people of Nazareth are in agreement that you can be received back into the community if you agree."

I fought disappointment as my wedding dreams faded. My friends would not be there to celebrate; there would be no elaborate wedding garments and lengthy preparations. I nodded my head, eyes down.

"Thank you, Abba," I spoke respectfully, knowing that there was no other way.

"Thank Joseph," Abba responded. "He has taken great risks on your behalf, Mary. He spoke in length with Gad. We owe him a great debt of gratitude and you owe him your life."

The men left the room and Elizabeth took the baby to her mattress to nurse.

"I brought something for you," Ima said, approaching me with a package. She handed me a bundle wrapped in silk boasting all the blues of the sky at dawn. I unwrapped it to find that the cloth was an exquisite shawl.

"How did you ever come across something so beautiful," I gasped.

Ima smiled and pointed to the corner where silver tassels hung. and the words of the prophet Isaiah were embroidered into the hem of the fabric, *"Instead of your shame you will receive a double portion, and instead of disgrace you will rejoice in your inheritance. And so you will inherit a double portion in your land, and everlasting joy will be yours.*[29] "

I didn't know what to say. Ima shook out the shawl and draped my head as a veil.

"You will be a beautiful bride," she smiled. "The Lord has taken away your shame."

"Look, there's more," she added, pulling out her own wedding dress from the package. I have made adjustments so that it fits you.

"Thank you, Ima," I murmured, taking her hand in mine. Her slender fingers were marked with age, my own looked pale and fragile next to hers.

I tried to show my appreciation for how much she had sacrificed to give me these gifts, but my heart ached.

Seventeen

I sat in the corner with John who lay kicking his legs and gurgling. I picked up a cloth and hung it gently over his face, pulling it down his body, which made him blink and squirm. I smiled. Elizabeth's house buzzed with activity. Joseph had returned to Nazareth to make final preparations and to accompany Gad on his journey to Elizabeth's house. Having a Rabbi from Elizabeth's town to conduct the ceremony would arouse too much suspicion. Jewish weddings were usually large and loud occasions, and anyway, I was already showing. I placed my hands on my small round belly and wondered why God would want his son to be born this way. I sighed then laughed. John was working his arms and legs so intently to get my attention that he looked like a bug on its back.

"Here Mary, tie these garlands," instructed Ima, handing me a handful of dried flowers and linen.

"Why are you doing all of this, Ima?" I asked, unable to hide my disappointment.

She laid down a handful of fabric and squatted in front of me.

"You are my daughter. These might not have been the circumstances we would have chosen for your wedding but these are the ones we have. We can wallow, or we can celebrate."

She went back to her tasks. Should it be such an easy choice? I was surrounded by people who loved me dearly. I was preparing to marry the man I loved and I was carrying a miracle. My name would be known for generations to come. I had been charged with raising this child who would be the Messiah, the savior of the world. So why? Why was it so hard? Did it simply come down to expectations? Certainly I would never have expected to marry this way, or to bring my child into the world under such threat. So who was I disappointed in? Myself? God perhaps; yet what right did I have to place expectations on God?

John began to cry. I rose to my feet and picked him up. The blanket swaddled his little body and I rocked him, soothed him, eyes drooping, body relaxing. His wails subsided as sleep took over and he let go. Trust.

I laid him in his cradle and started work on the garlands as Ima had asked. What would trust require? What else could be lost? He had not spared my suffering but he had spared my life. The road I had already walked had been excruciating. Would the cost be greater still? Could I bare it? I did not know.

For the next week, Ima and Elizabeth cleaned, baked, arranged and sewed. They were like best friends reunited, never a pause between them. Our meal times were filled with love and conversation, each meal a feast. I had never eaten so well. Abba constructed a small *chuppah* for the ceremony and accompanied Zechariah on his tasks during the day leaving the women to their chores. Zechariah made up for the many months of silence and filled the home with fun. He carried a great depth that I admired. He was so proud of his son and spoke to him as if he were already a man; making plans for the future and explaining tasks, ideas and thoughts in great detail. I stayed in the home but left the women to their tasks unless they asked specifically for help. I preferred to hold John who could entertain me for hours with each turn of his head and blink of his eyes. I soaked in his fresh baby scent, wiped the milk from his mouth and kissed his tears away.

Elizabeth sat beside me one afternoon when Ima went with Abba and Zechariah to the synagogue. She carried a new vigor, uncharacteristic of a woman her age. Many were stooped and fragile but she had lost 30 years with the child. She sat comfortably beside me and reached for the boy who was already heavy in my arms, lifting him easily. He gazed into her eyes, knowing her and reached to be nursed, instincts sharp. She arranged him carefully, stroking his little curls and tucking in hands that only wanted to be free.

"This child does not want to be caressed," she laughed. "I think he will keep me running for many years to come." Her eyes were bright, the lines on her face beautiful. One moment, one miracle, one touch was all it had taken to erase her years of sorrow. As John drifted into sleep, Elizabeth turned to me and reached for my hand.

"I have watched you for many weeks, Hamuda." She tried to make me look at her while she spoke but I distracted myself with the loose fabric of my tunic.

"Something bothers you still, and will not let you go. Speak to me, Mary. Maybe I can help you carry this burden and God willing, He will take it from you."

"How did you keep loving God when He had taken so much from you?" I asked tentatively. I was afraid to speak so boldly, afraid to offend God.

Elizabeth smiled softly, nodding and taking her time to respond.

"We must never be led to believe that the present holds the final answer. *God chose the foolish things of the world to shame the wise; He chose the weak things of the world to shame the strong.*[30] You will discover that the ways of God are not the ways of the world. You must learn to look beyond."

I sat, waiting for her to continue but instead, she sat patiently waiting for me.

"Savta…. she wanted to get rid of the baby."

"Yes," Elizabeth responded gently. "And what about you?"

Months of emotion surged up like an uncovered well, and poured into her lap.

"I thought about it," I cried. "I was so afraid. I didn't know what to do and I just wanted …."

My voice trailed and Elizabeth sat silently stroking my hair. She did not speak, allowing me the time to exhaust tears.

"Have you spoken to God about this?" she asked as my sobs began to subside.

"I can't," I responded, horrified at the thought. "I have

disgraced him."

"What do you think He would do?" she asked.

"I don't know," I whispered, shrugging shoulders and wringing hands.

She tightened her embrace around me.

"Are you shocked?" I asked.

"I knew as soon as you walked in the door," she answered. "The Spirit of God had fallen on me with joy and spoke to my heart that He would turn your mourning into laughter. You must forgive yourself, Mary."

"I can't."

"Are you angry?" she asked.

I gasped, her words like a sword.

"Yes!" I stiffened and words flew.

"Everyone betrayed me. They almost killed me!" She waited for me to go on.

"Everyone turned their back on me. I don't know how to let go of this pain."

"Is that it?" she asked.

I shook my head.

"Who are you really angry with?"

"Myself," I sobbed. "I wanted to die. I wanted my baby to die."

I gulped for air, face hot, body rigid. I clutched at my tunic to pull it away from my neck. Elizabeth rushed for water.

"None of this is a surprise to Him." Elizabeth spoke firmly now. "The battle for life is not one to be taken lightly. Darkness always leans to death and we are pulled along by it. The struggle you have faced is not in resisting darkness but in choosing the light. Today, you have chosen, Mary. You have nothing to be ashamed of. Your brokenness is all that is necessary."

It felt as though oil was being poured over me. It poured over my head and shoulders, down my body and streamed in rivulets over my feet and onto the floor. Eyes closed, shaky hands fallen by my side, I let it wash over and inside, cleaning out. I smelled the same smell of love that knew my sin from the beginning of time but chose me anyway; the look of love that could see beyond.

I now had to make the choice to see myself as God saw me and not through the lens of failure that sentenced me to justice. His mercy washed and I chose to exchange everything for the promise. I could not know what tomorrow would hold. I could not anticipate what others might say or do but I was no longer a victim of my circumstances, of rejection and betrayal. As I forgave them, and finally forgave myself, chains unlocked and fell to the ground. Love unhindered poured in.

Eighteen

Morning broke fierce with love, my heart swelled with new freedom. The noise of the city that had once been so unfamiliar now brought reassurance. Sounds of work and play, idle chatter and business dealings swirled in the dawn. My life had broadened here and what was once unknown and to be feared had brought untold possibilities.

Ima and Elizabeth had been up long before sunrise. I did not feel tired despite a fitful sleep. I wanted desperately to see Joseph again but was anxious about the meeting with Gad. I would have been happy if I never saw him again and hoped that he would not spoil what little celebration was left for my wedding. I joined the women and ate in silence, receiving their kisses and getting caught up in the excitement. Tables were laid and plates positioned ready to receive roasted vegetables, fruits, olives and flat breads, oils, fish and lamb, pine nuts and *kugel* and more desserts than we could ever eat. Flowers spilled over platters and candles stood proudly waiting to be lit.

"Come Mary," Ima took my hand and helped me to my feet. The breakfast had been cleared away and I looked curiously at these women who were as giddy as little girls. She led me outside where the cool morning air wrapped its chill around us in welcome. We took the stairs up to the roof.

"Oh Ima, it's stunning," I exclaimed as we reached the top. The roof had been transformed from a meager gathering place to a decadent garden. Trellises lined the ledge and crawled with flowers and vines. A tub where I would bathe for the traditional wedding purification had replaced the old rain barrel. Fabric draped between the trellises and over the tub, while candles flickered, illuminating every dim corner. Cloths were neatly folded on a small table that held oils and perfumes. I threw my arms around her and clung until Elizabeth alighted.

"Enough of that, we've plenty to get done today," she teased, squeezing our arms. The three of us embraced. The sun inched its way upwards exchanging pink for gold and casting its warmth on our faces.

"Ima thought of everything," Elizabeth spoke gently, turning me around to point out every detail. "Each element is symbolic, Mary, and representative of the *great cloud of witnesses*[31] that surrounds and applauds you today. My head swam with the fragrance of so many flowers. Grapes hung heavy and bowls of nuts and fruit sat waiting to be eaten.

"Thank you," I whispered to Ima.

She took my hand and Elizabeth took the other. We closed our eyes as she prayed the *marriage prayer*, *'May it be Your will, Adonai, that this marriage shall prosper. May theirs be a harmonious union of love and togetherness, peace and friendship, a union which is in accord with the law of Moses and Judaism; a fitting union, permeated with fear of God and fear of sin; a marriage blessed with good and righteous children; a blessed union, wherein there may be fulfilled through Mary the verse, 'Your wife shall be as a fruitful vine within your house; your children like olive shoots around your table*[32]*.' May theirs be a union wherein her husband shall take delight in her more than in all worldly delights, as is written, 'Houses and riches are inherited from parents, but a prudent wife is from the Lord*[33]*.' "*

"Take your time," she added as they left me alone.

I sat on a low stool to drink in the beauty. I pulled the fabric so that the space would be completely enclosed and waited as the holiness of the moment descended. Finally, I undressed and slipped into the tub sinking down and letting the water glide over my head. I opened my eyes looking through the surface, colors and shapes moving and shifting. I came up for air and closed my eyes reciting the *Bride's Tefillah*, 'Baruch Atah Ado-nai Elo-heinu Melech HaOlam Asher Kidishanu B'mitzvotav V'tzivanu Al Hatevilah. We bless you, God, Our God, Ruler of the Universe who has made us holy by commanding the immersion.'

I stayed a while, just waiting, soaking, listening. New robes hung over the tub and I dried and dressed. The sheets danced in the breeze and I stretched my arms wide. Large clouds, full of morning, puffed lazily across the azure sky. I tilted my head back, breathing deep of joy and certainty. Thoughts floated through my mind; thoughts of painful past, thoughts of fearful future but they evaporated in the assurance of here and now.

"You are here, God. I know it." Tears trickled back from corners of eyes and ran down tender neck. "Why is it so hard to stay in this place, in this knowledge?"

I lifted my arms high, heart filled with love. This was where I wanted to remain. Peace.

I made my way downstairs, startled by a chicken that had roosted in the eaves. It squawked at me before flying haphazardly, crash landing and scuttling away.

"Will you help me?" I asked Ima as I entered the house, the bottles of oil and perfume clustered in my arms.

She smiled and laid down her work to sit and comb, applying the oils to my hair, skin and nails. Elizabeth braided and pinned my long hair; loose tresses hanging and adorned with frangipane blossoms. John cooed and kicked his legs by my side. He resisted the swaddling cloths, preferring to kick and punch at the air, already asserting his unwillingness to conform.

We ate lunch in wistful quiet. Hearts knit in joyful anticipation. Ima rose and sang softly as she hung the dress. The bright light of early afternoon moved delicately across the walls and over the dress as I watched. The passing of time made me nervous and excited. There was still a part of me that wished I could stay with Abba and Ima, finding safety in what I already knew, and yet stepping into this unknown would be safer still.

As the hour approached, Ima carried the dress and draped it over my hands, lifted high. I let the cool fabric sweep down over my body and land perfectly over every curve. Ima and Elizabeth fussed and scurried, fastening buttons, smoothing folds and fixing my hair. The dress was made of simple white linen that circled delicately around my neck.

The sleeves were elegantly embroidered with silver stitching and reached to my wrists. Ima had made adjustments so that it hung discreetly over my expanding belly and flowed in ripples to the floor. A simple silver sash crossed my shoulder and tied at the waist. I dared not move in case I wrinkled the fabric as I waited anxiously for Joseph to arrive. At the sound of his footsteps my heart pounded. Instead of a veil, Ima pulled the blue silk shawl low over my eyes and laid the tassels over my shoulders and down the front of the dress.

Zechariah entered first and escorted Gad to the chuppah, a symbol of the home that Joseph and I would share. Abba and Zechariah had cut and tied tree branches in a makeshift covering that Ima draped with Abba's old prayer shawl that I remembered from childhood. It was primitive and not like the large and ornate chuppahs from most weddings, but it was adequate. My eyes scanned each curve and knot of the poles, and then I saw that Joseph had carved small flowers and inscribed the wood making it more personal and intimate than any I had seen.

Zechariah's silence leant sobriety to the event as his voice had brought much joy to our gatherings over the last weeks. We were stilled by the awe of Presence ushered in.

Abba's eyes were moist as he approached; unable to speak he took my hand and squeezed in response to my smile. I waited and watched the door, shifting from one foot to the other. The light of sun that had streamed into the room was momentarily overshadowed as Joseph entered. His long Passover robe draped over shoulders and cascaded to his feet. His prayer shawl hung almost to the ground, blue stripes vivid against the rich white fabric. I was unable to see anything other than his robes until he lifted the shawl from my eyes. My face tingled as his hands came close. His eyes shone, laden with love and for a brief moment, there was just the two of us. He lowered the shawl and took my arm, guiding me under the chuppah where Gad began the ceremonial singing of the Torah. His voice was thick, beautiful. The melody rang softly around the room and the air became heavy. I soaked in every moment; even the silence seemed to be filled with angelic voices. The ketubah that we had signed at our betrothal lay on a dressed table before us. All that had transpired since that day was laid to rest as I looked into Joseph's eyes and we began again. He took my hand and pressed a special coin into my palm. This gift had been passed down through his family from the time of David. I closed my fingers over it embracing history, significance, the blessing of this man and of the many gifts that had been placed in my life. The baby in my womb turned, giving me secret reassurance of the gift of his presence. Joseph offered me the cup of wine. My acceptance sealed our covenant and Zechariah broke the intensity of the moment when he called out '*Mazal Tov*!' making us all laugh.

I looked at Gad who placed the glass on the floor for Joseph to smash underfoot. I wondered why he had made such a journey for us. I had not looked him in the eye when he entered the room but as Joseph smashed the cup and the room became alive with joy, we shared a moment of unspoken understanding, forgiveness perhaps, or maybe compassion. Either way his look was tender towards me. Everyone called out 'Mazel Tov!' Zechariah looking sheepish at his haste earlier. A whirlwind of celebration erupted as we embraced and gathered in a circle where we danced until we could not stand. Elizabeth brought out the food and we spent the evening feasting together. The day was perfect and instead of grand celebration, it was closeness and intimacy that set it apart.

Joseph pulled me aside as the men dismantled the chuppah and the women cleared the table. He touched my hair, twisting the ends through his fingers.

"You are beautiful in every way, my true love. There is no flaw in you.[34]*"*

His words wrapped around my heart, the heat of breath on my cheek as he whispered words of love.

"I must go, Mary. We must not be together until the child is born." He sighed deeply and ran his hand through his carefully combed hair. The tousled curls that I was used to returned. I took his hand and kissed his palm, knowing that this would be a night of longing. He turned and disappeared. I stood alone, dress wrinkled now. Just a child; now mother and wife.

Nineteen

The following day, we began our final preparations to leave. Elizabeth was fully recovered after the birth and the baby was thriving. It was time to go home. I felt more confident after seeing Gad as I knew that we would be received back into Nazareth. Joseph had said nothing to me about the reactions of our neighbors when he had returned after bringing me here. I could only imagine the speculation and rumors following my abrupt disappearance, especially as Joseph and I were both due to stand trial just days after my departure. Somehow, a resolution had been reached with the village elders. But how would my friends react? I knew that we would likely be greeted cordially and received back into society, but what would happen at the well, or behind my back? Would my name be protected? My heart raced at the thought of the many encounters I would have that would be overshadowed. Would my friends allow their children to play with mine?

We gathered our supplies and prepared food for the long journey. The weather had begun to cool slightly and I hoped it would be more bearable than our journey here. Gad had left early in the morning to join a caravan that was heading north and would return him home quicker than we could manage. We remained for one more day so that we could celebrate the Shabbat meal together. Elizabeth had baked sweet *challah* loaves and we filled our bellies with roast chicken and vegetable soup, barley, *matza* balls and wine from the vineyards.

"What extraordinary days are upon us!" exclaimed Zechariah. "If you had told me one year ago that I would be sharing Shabbat with you under these circumstances I would have cursed you for blasphemy."

We laughed halfheartedly; the reality of the many curses already bestowed dampened the humor.

"We must realize," he went on solemnly, "that the extraordinary is not reserved for those who are extraordinary. These days are such because of He who has chosen the ordinary in which to display His splendor. We must not despise the path before us though many do not understand. Walk forward confidently, for surely there are many more extraordinary days ahead."

We rested on the Sabbath and then rose early the following morning to depart. The moment was bittersweet. All that I had received at Elizabeth's house had restored my soul and healed my crushed heart. I was able to look forward confidently even though our goodbyes were filled with sorrow.

"I am here for you always, Hamuda," Elizabeth spoke as she squeezed me tightly. I took the baby from her arms and kissed him over and over until he squealed for his mother. I giggled, thankful for the diversion from my tears. Zechariah placed his hands on our heads and declared the joy of the Lord over our lives and marriage. His hands shook with fervency until Joseph, laughing, finally placed them back by Zechariah's side.

"Enough, Uncle. We don't want Mary to go into labor just yet."

Joseph helped me onto the donkey and tied our belongings in front and behind to give me some support. Abba and Ima led the way and we took our time behind them, negotiating the rocky terrain as we traversed the steep hill down to the road. We talked little at first, the awkwardness of our love still standing between us; Joseph walked closely beside me, his shoulder frequently brushing my knees. I wanted to reach my hand into his thick, dark hair but I resisted even though there was no one around to see. The hours rolled by and conversation began to flow. We talked of John and anticipated the birth of our son. Joseph's pride was evident as he planned to teach the child his trade and raise him to know the scriptures. He spoke of fishing in the Galilee and of trips together to the temple. We dreamed that day, and it was good.

We all stopped together in the shade for lunch. The figs were ripe and dropped around us with a shake of the branches. We ate hungrily, the abundance of sweet fruit reenergizing us for the road ahead. Abba and Ima went on and I decided to walk for a while. Joseph put his arm around my shoulders to keep me from stumbling. The sun was at its hottest and although it didn't compare with the oppressive heat of summer, we were thankful for any shade we could find.

"Abba told me that you spoke to Gad about our return to Nazareth," I spoke, hoping that he would indulge my request for conversation.

Joseph nodded but did not speak.

"You have saved my life twice now, and the life of our child," I went on. "I am forever in your debt."

"You owe me nothing," Joseph responded. "It was my duty and privilege to protect you."

He stopped, face lined with weariness.

"Your acceptance of me, your love and the gift of this child are more than I ever thought I could have again. I did not want to lose you, Mary. My heart was broken with grief; my purpose shattered, but God has restored more than life to me. The only debt that is owed is to Him."

The sound of women washing clothes by the river diverted my attention. Their voices rang in unison as songs rose spontaneously from hearts, and invited others around to join in. The sound of the wet clothes beating rhythmically on the rocks set the cadence for their melodies. I looked at Joseph as he took my hand in his; we walked on.

We traveled for many days; moving east to avoid Samaria as we had heard that there was much unrest there. The extended journey was hard but at least we were safe. We trekked north to Tiberias, caught between rugged hills and the beauty of the Jordan River, stopping only to eat or set up our tents for the night. As we reached Galilee, we followed the road west for the last part of our journey.

A commotion ahead caused us to stop and find refuge

in an orchard.

"Stay here with the women," Joseph spoke to Abba. "I'll go and look over the hill and see what is happening."

It felt as though he was gone for hours and yet the sun stood still overhead. Rushing back, he took the donkey's reigns hurriedly.

"We must move quickly. The soldiers are marching this way; this could mean trouble."

We doubled back until we found a small side road that would take us slightly north through Cana and Sephoris where we could find a south road to Nazareth. We walked silently with constant glances over our shoulders until we were certain that we were out of harms way. I didn't want to go near Sephoris but there was no other way home. I had always loved this ancient city, 'the Jewel of Galilee'. Its fame traveled far and its beauty had often beckoned us to make the one-hour walk from home. When it was taken over by the Romans we kept our distance, always hoping that one day the city would be reclaimed. Our path would lead us right up to its gate and around its wall as we traveled south to home. I had only been gone for a few months but already I could feel a shift in atmosphere. Herod the Great had visited and brought his insanity with him. Tension was building; fear was prevalent and the Jews who lived in or near Sephoris were never able to let down their guard. We rounded the corner of a small hill, the path leading down toward the great walls that loomed below. Large crowds had gathered, shouting, jeering, screaming. I shuddered and the donkey panicked, resisting Joseph's hold on the reigns. It took several minutes to calm him down. Abba and Joseph spoke hurriedly to make a decision. We could not turn back and risk an encounter with the soldiers, but we could not determine what had caused such a mob.

"Perhaps we can make our way around without being noticed," said Abba.

"Perhaps," Joseph replied quietly, deep in thought. "Either way poses danger. We will press on and hope to avoid attention."

We moved towards the edge of the crowd. Most of the people congregated on the hillside, their focus away from the city. With dismay, we noticed that soldiers were gathered there too. As we descended the hill, the fresh air filled with the smell of sacrifice. I gagged and covered my mouth and nose with my shawl. We kept our eyes down. Hundreds of people swarmed ahead, jostling and pushing aggressively. We moved slowly as more people joined.

"Get out of the way," a man spoke gruffly as he stumbled drunkenly across the path, frightening the donkey and shoving Joseph.

I grabbed the donkey's mane, letting my shawl drop away from my face. The smells were unreal, I could hardly breathe. Faint, I reached out for Joseph and looked out across the crowd, my eyes raised from the road momentarily. Death hung twitching on trees. I gasped at the horror; I had heard of it but had only seen it in my nightmares. I slid off the donkey and buried my head in Joseph's tunic but the image was already burned in my mind. At least ten men were strung up on crosses; their arms bound so tightly that the ropes cut into their flesh making hands turn purple. Metal nails as big as the pins used for chariot wheels had been hammered through their wrists so that their fingers curled and contorted. Their feet were stacked one on top of the other with a spike driven through. Blood from their wounds and from lashings with the whip ran down the wooden crosses and pooled on the ground. The throng mocked the men who hung naked, gasping for breath and begging for mercy. One of the soldiers took a club and beat the man that was crying out. He beat him until the bones in his knees broke so that he could not push himself up to take a breath. I could not look but heard his last desperate breaths as he suffocated.

Joseph shuffled me between himself and the donkey so that I would be hidden. We made our way silently, our clothes torn by cacti that lined the road. We neared the city walls; tension rife. Small groups united, only to be dispersed by soldiers who flaunted their weapons. We moved quickly, sometimes trapped between the hordes and the walls of the city. Finally we made our way through. As I looked up, I saw the buzzards circling, waiting for the crowd to disperse so that they could have their fill of last week's corpses that hung rotting, waiting to be devoured. Rome was beside itself with blood lust and driven by the sickness of a man so depraved that he had ordered the death of his own sons and smirked as he watched them die. There was no limit.

"You!" someone behind us called out.

"Keep your head down," said Joseph. He tightened his grip on me and the donkey's bridle. We moved forward a little faster, jostling enough to get through but hoping not to draw attention.

"You! Stop!" the man called out again. Agitation charged the air.

"Is he calling us?" I asked Joseph in a panic.

"Just keep going," he said. I don't know who he wants but perhaps we can lose him.

Suddenly, the man was upon us, he grabbed Joseph's shoulder and spun him around. The force almost knocked me off my feet but Joseph caught me. His eyes blazed but he remained calm.

"What do you want?" he asked.

"Do you not remember me?" the man replied sarcastically. I commissioned work from you and you cheated me out of my money.

"I do remember you," Joseph responded. "I did not cheat you. The work was completed by Avi when I was unable to finish the job."

"Ah yes, Avi." He rubbed his face to calm a violent spasm and then pushed Joseph backwards, his face still convulsing. "Like I said, you cheated me. You handed me over for second class work so you could go off with this piece of work and her bastard child."

Joseph seethed, his fists ready for a fight. All attention turned towards us, licking lips in anticipation of free entertainment.

"Please Joseph," I croaked. "God will defend us."

The man pushed Joseph again, pressing him for retaliation. It took all of Joseph's self-control to turn his back on his aggressor. The mob closed in, men eager to get in on the action. Joseph grabbed me and pushed me to the ground as a club swung over our heads and hit the man square in the jaw. Blood splattered around us as the riot broke loose. We scrambled to freedom, the donkey braying and kicking men out of our way. We ran for our lives and fled from the city until we were forced to stop for breath.

"Are you hurt?" Joseph demanded, his hands smoothing my hair and turning my face this way and that looking for signs of injury. He took a piece of cloth and wiped the blood splatters off my cheek.

"I'm fine," I gasped. Adrenaline coursed and my abdomen strained with the weight of the child.

I looked over my shoulder to the city where soldiers had dispersed the pack with their own madness. Abba and Ima had managed to get through faster than us and we could see them waiting on the road ahead. Joseph waved them on, reassuring them that we were safe and not wanting to concern them. They waved back and turned to continue their journey.

"Let's just keep going," I urged.

We moved slowly. The end was close but still seemed so far away, each step intentional. I wanted to distract myself from all that we had seen. Joseph's broad shoulders sagged. His pace had slowed, his feet torn with blisters. We were both weary and this last ordeal had taken its toll. I searched for a diversion, something to pass the time as we approached home.

"Tell me how you swayed the decision of Gad and the elders concerning me," I probed.

"It's not important," he said gruffly.

"They wanted to kill me, Joseph. I can't imagine what you said to them. Gad even seemed happy to be at our wedding." I pressed him, my emotions almost getting the better of me.

He wound the bridle tightly around his hand and arm, the worn leather strap cracked under the pressure as his fingers flexed and clenched. The donkey brayed, as he was pulled off center. I stroked his mane and clicked my tongue to soothe him and wished that I had said nothing.

Twenty

I clambered back onto the donkey, Joseph assisting. I had ridden and walked alternately as my condition dictated. I could not sit for long but neither could I walk without becoming light headed. We were so close to home; the sun cast an ethereal glow on the rocks and threw ribbons of amber clouds across the horizon. I rested my hand on Joseph's shoulder and he glanced at me, then at the donkey that panted with exhaustion. We stopped while Joseph gave him a drink. I shifted in my seat to find a more comfortable position; my belly forced me upright so that every movement jolted, with little room to compensate. I bit my lip, desperate to find a place to lie down and take the pressure off my back.

We walked on in silence. The sounds of Sephoris ebbed in the background and daylight settled into dusk. Lizards scurried to their rocks and birds flocked to roost leaving the space before us empty for night to fall. My head bobbed as my eyes tried to close. The slip of the reigns from my hands would wake me with a start only to realize that barely ten steps had passed. I groaned but regretted it as Joseph turned, reaching out to me with concern.

"Mary, are you in pain?" he asked tenderly.

I think he would have carried me.

"I'll be fine, Joseph. I'm just so tired."

I reached down and placed my hands on his beard, lifting his face. He covered my slender hands with his.

"You are so good to me," I spoke.

His eyes, red from lack of sleep, reached out to my soul. How much more could this girl child handle?

"I'm fine, Joseph," I echoed.

He nodded, taking a breath, clearing his mind. He patted the donkey to urge him forward and we walked steadily on.

"You must understand that it was the only way. You must not take it to heart, Mary." His voice revealed no sorrow.

"What is it?" I asked cautiously.

"Tell me that you will take my words objectively," he spoke firmly. "The situation was grave, Mary; you know that. I prayed for many hours about how I was to speak to the elders. I could not go to them with a simple plea. It would have been a mockery. All sides were urging me to choose my freedom over your life. No judge would have refused me. Even the Torah laid out my course."

"I understand, Joseph," I said, confident in my husband's wisdom.

"I spoke to them of Hosea, the prophet. God commanded him to take a prostitute as his wife. Their marriage was a symbol of God's covenant with Israel who had been unfaithful to Him, following other gods and breaking the commandments. God wanted to show how far he would go to rescue."

He turned to look up at me, brow furrowed.

"I told them that perhaps you were like Israel, and that I was like Hosea. Even if you were a whore, I was willing to marry you."

The very word that had been used against me by the soldier, the very word that had condemned me to death had now saved my life.

"They see me as your redeemer, Mary, and they have accepted us for the sake of Israel and her infidelity." He drew himself closer so that our faces were just inches apart and dropped his voice to a whisper.

"Take heart, my love. Take hold of hope. Hosea's prophecy ends with a declaration that one day God will renew His covenant with His people and take Israel back in love. Who knows? Perhaps we are part of this story."

He wiped a tear from my face, then turned south. His chest lifted. Carefully unwinding the cloth that sheltered his head from the sun, he wiped his brow which glistened in the evening light. The sound of locusts rose up out of the stillness. I looked up the hill where the goats were being led back to Nazareth.

"Shalom!" called the shepherd, waving, and then chasing a stray animal.

My focus turned towards home. I longed to see the familiar sights of childhood and to settle into my new life but I knew nothing of what that life held. I was thankful that night was upon us. Most people would be in their homes and

I hoped that we could travel unnoticed through the streets. We climbed the steep hill steadily; even the donkey had lost its motivation. Joseph stopped to collect water from the well as we made our way silently through the village.

Our new home sat on the west side of Nazareth overlooking the hills and giving us some sense of solitude. The inside was much the same as Abba and Ima's house, except that Joseph had his carpenter's shop built on to the left side of the house. On the right was a simple wooden shelter where he tied the donkey for the night. My back throbbed and I slid clumsily to the ground. Joseph helped me into the house and pulled out a mat so that I could sit. He lit and hung a lamp and started a fire to heat the vegetable soup that Ima had set out for us. Despite their age, they had made the final journey much quicker than us. Joseph unburdened the donkey and unpacked our belongings while I watched. I set the loaf of bread on a blanket with a selection of dried fruit, olives and grapes that were left over from the trip. Joseph brought pomegranates in from the tree outside. We were exhausted and sore.

"You must sleep now." Joseph got up and laid a blanket on my bed in the corner.

"I will sleep on the roof," he added.

"Please, Joseph," I pleaded. "You don't have to. You can just make your bed on the other side of the room," I suggested.

"No, I must." His tone was harsh and I wondered what had come over him.

He waited until I was settled and then disappeared up the ladder and through the hatch to the roof. I tossed and turned throughout the night, wishing that Joseph was by my side. I had become more accustomed to the sounds of the city than I had realized. The darkness and silence of Nazareth that I had always known was unnerving.

I woke up late in the morning and adjusted to my new surroundings. There was little work to be done. Joseph had prepared the home for us before our wedding. Newly built stools and a table were set in place and all the pots and jugs that I would ever require lined the wall. I swept and put the food away, then hung a blanket around my bed where I could change discreetly. I combed and braided my hair; singing songs that I hoped would give me courage. Joseph had set out food for breakfast and I could hear him outside. I washed quickly and then went out to find him.

"Joseph," I spoke softly so that I didn't startle him.

He turned and we greeted each other.

"Did you eat the food I left out?" he asked.

"No, I thought we would eat together," I answered.

"I ate already," he replied but, sensing my disappointment, he added, "we will eat together tonight."

"Very good," I said, turning to observe the workers down in the field. I must join them soon but I hoped that I could wait a little longer.

"I will fetch supplies and water today."

I wanted to receive some direction, or at least some encouragement but Joseph just nodded and returned to his shop. The pounding of tools gave me a headache. I went and sat on the hillside where I would be undisturbed. If I waited long enough, I could fetch water and supplies without meeting many of the villagers who would be busy with work or in their homes. For two weeks I was able to avoid contact with anyone I knew closely. Even on the Sabbath, Joseph went alone to the synagogue as I had woken up with sickness and was not able to rise from my bed. By the afternoon I felt much better and I saw the suspicion in his eyes.

"You can't avoid people forever, Mary," he spoke with an edge of frustration.

"I know," I sighed. "But how do I face them? I don't know who my friends are any more. I don't know if I have friends. It is easier to stay here."

"Of course," he replied. "But hiding does not solve the problem; it just gives more room for speculation to grow. Your friends will be those who do not judge."

All that I had known before was gone forever. A new path was being forged before me; every step was risk and required more of me than I thought I could stand.

"Why don't you go and see Ima," Joseph encouraged. "It will do you good."

Ima, I had missed her so much since we had returned. She had not been to visit, leaving me the space to be a new wife and yet I longed to see her. Joseph set his hammer on the bench. His shop was small but well organized. Every inch of space was used. Tools were mounted on walls or hung from the ceiling. Wood chips and dust coated the floor, covering his feet. The smell of fresh lumber coated my tongue.

"I will go with you."

He made his way around the bench towards me, wiping the dust off his face with his apron.

"I don't mean to disturb you," I added.

"You are not disturbing me. I will walk with you."

"Perhaps we should go the long way, around the back of the village," I suggested. I knew that there would be a crowd collecting water.

"No," he replied. "We will walk by the well. You have

nothing to fear. Their thoughts of you belong to them. You must not take possession of them."

We walked on, our arms touching but not entwined. My gaze met the floor whenever we passed a neighbor.

"Look up, Mary," Joseph commanded quietly.

Each man that we passed greeted Joseph respectfully. I wanted to cry. We entered the courtyard, the synagogue welcoming on the far side. The market bustled and boasted the colors and scents of the best of Galilee. The well hummed with activity. Little girls walked by with jugs of water nestled on shoulders or balanced carefully on their heads. Livestock ran around chased by children. I heard the whispers of women before we reached them.

"Greet them," Joseph said.

"I can't," I whispered.

"You must. They don't know what to say to you. You must make an effort."

My hands shook and I hid them beneath the folds of my tunic so no one would see. I looked up at them all staring at me.

"Hello." I couldn't hide the nervousness in my voice. I looked at them, one by one; my friends, playmates, aunts and cousins; suddenly so distant.

They murmured hellos in response, looking first at us, then at each other and finally returning their attention back to the well. We were about to continue past them when my dear friend Sari approached. Her eyes filled with tears.

"I am so happy to see you, Mary. I have been worried." She kissed my cheek and then returned to the well. A ripple of indecision rolled through the group and then one by one, the women came. Some kissed me; others took my hand or just spoke their greeting. It was difficult but my heart was moved. Joseph stood stoically beside me, nodding at each as they approached.

We walked on and I was relieved to reach Ima's house and close the door. She hugged me and told me to sit.

"I will go and see Joachim," said Joseph. "I will return for you at dinner." He placed a hand on my shoulder. "You did well today."

I smiled, surprised at the relief that his words gave me. The baby kicked my ribs, causing me to shift position.

"How are you feeling, Mary? Is the child being good to you?" asked Ima with a twinkle in her eye. "I remember when I was expecting you. I loved feeling you squirm and move around."

I rubbed my belly. I loved the feeling too.

"Ima, do you think I'm crazy?" I asked.

"Why would I think that?" she replied without looking up, her hands working the grinding stone.

"The angel. Perhaps it was just a dream."

Ima laughed. "A dream that came true? I think I would rather believe that you saw an angel."

Twenty-one

I leaned into pillows, watching her work and enjoying home again.

"Life has certainly taken a turn around here," she said in response to my insecurity. "I don't think anything would surprise me anymore."

She looked up from the mill and sat back, brushing hair from eyes. Ima was beautiful. She was delicate, her frame small; nose sculpted and lips like lily petals. Her eyes were large and shaped like tear drops. Long eyelashes and strong brows framed her face and I pictured the beauty of her youth. I wished that I looked more like her but I resembled Abba. I had Ima's hair though. Hers was grey and thin now but I remember as a child watching her brush locks that reached down her back. Mine too had grown thick and strong. It tumbled and caught the rays of the sun making streaks of light appear in the blackness. My crown.

"Mary, when you first told me that you were pregnant I was shocked, but you must remember that a great deal happened very quickly. There was little time to process all that was occurring. I never doubted you and yet I could never have been prepared for the situation that was suddenly thrown upon us. My reaction, or perhaps it was my lack of a response, hurt you. I wanted to let Joachim lead us through as I was afraid that I might say or do something that would cause you more danger. I was concerned for your life and reason left me."

I accepted her words. It was pointless to go back and consider what could or should have been done differently. Ima and I had never been as close as some of the other girls with their mothers, our relationship largely functional. She taught me the role of women and I helped her bake and grind the flour. We rarely shared deeply so I often kept my thoughts and feelings to myself. I knew that she loved me but my confidence had always been in Abba and she seemed to be satisfied with that. I picked up a basket and began to sort grains, conversation over, but Ima went on.

"I must share something with you that I have never told you before," she added. "I have not spoken of this for many years but now it would benefit you to know."

I inched forward with surprise and interest.

"When Joachim and I married, I longed for a child. The years passed by and I watched my friends marry and bear child after child. My heart broke and I wept many lonely tears. Each time that we traveled to Jerusalem to go to the

Temple, we would make a detour to Zechariah and Elizabeth's house and then make the rest of the journey together. Elizabeth and I were a source of strength and comfort to each other. No one else could identify with our suffering but saw us as cursed by God." She paused, the wound still not entirely healed.

This insight into Ima's life before I was born opened my heart to her. This woman, strong and capable was showing me her pain. I had not considered this before.

"Elizabeth and I spent many hours together praying and seeking the Lord for our plight. We cried out for mercy and spoke to each other the stories of Sarah, Rebekah, Rachel and Hannah, all of whom had conceived miraculously.

"Year after year we wailed and prayed. Soon our hope began to diminish as we were nearing the time when we would be too old to bear a child. My life was full but there was an emptiness in my heart that grew with each passing day. Elizabeth too bore her shame quietly. Zechariah continued to serve in the temple and Elizabeth served him. I counted myself blessed that I lived in a small community. Our circumstances were well known and so I rarely had to encounter a new situation that exposed my barrenness, but Elizabeth was faced with it daily and bore the scars of scorn.

"One year we had made the journey to the Temple for Passover. Joachim had entered the court with the other men and I stayed in the Court of Women. I loved the smells and atmosphere of Passover. Jerusalem was bursting at the seams with pilgrims, traders, rabbis and priests. Hundreds of thousands of livestock were herded through the gates to be presented as sacrifices. The aroma of bread baking, fresh spices and lamb roasting filled the air. There was no way to avoid the celebration, day or night, and no one wanted to.

Elizabeth was subdued but still participated. I had finally given up all hope and come to terms with my situation.

"I rose early one morning. The tents stretched far into the distance with barely room to negotiate a pathway. A lull had settled as everyone had finally crawled into bed leaving a few moments of quiet for me to enjoy alone. I picked my way over baskets and sleeping dogs and goats, trying not to cause anyone to wake up. I reached the city wall, vast to the east and west and enormous. I stood at its base and looked up. Huge stones towered and made me dizzy as they reached into the sky. I placed my hands on the cool rock to steady myself. I could hear the bustle and energy inside the walls as people began to stir. Slumber was still heavy behind me and I was caught in the stillness between sleeping and wakefulness. Suddenly, a light that was like nothing I had seen before blinded me. I turned my face as the brightness, in contrast to the shadow of early morning, stunned my eyes.

" 'What do you want with me?' I asked, petrified, in response to a voice that spoke out of the light.

" 'I am the Lord's messenger,' it said.

"The voice took shape and I looked into his eyes as he knelt before me.

" 'You will have your child,' he continued. 'She has been chosen from the beginning of time to fulfill the promise of Isaiah, *The virgin will be with child and will give birth to a son, and will call him Immanuel.*[35]'

"He did not stay long. He stood abruptly, throwing his head back and lifting his arms above his head and shouting,

" *'Salvation belongs to our God, who sits on the throne!*[36]'

"He drew his sword and thrust it into the air above him.

" *'Praise and glory and wisdom and thanks and honor and power and strength be to our God for ever and ever!*[37]

"With each word his sword reached higher and higher, and then he hurtled through the air like a star until he was no longer of this world.

"The coolness of the morning enveloped me as the sun rose and shed its light on my face. Its heat paled in comparison with the fire of Heaven. I could not contain my joy and I woke Joachim and Elizabeth to share the news. Joachim joined me in my delight but Elizabeth became sullen. I was consumed then by the celebrations surrounding me and the celebration inside. Nine months later I gave birth to you. Elizabeth would not talk to me about my experience and I never thought of the angel's words over the years, as your life was fulfillment enough. I hardly noticed Elizabeth's coldness at first as I was so absorbed, but the following year they did not travel with us to Jerusalem. She would not respond to any attempt I made to contact her and she would not see you. The first time she laid eyes on you was when you arrived at her house with Joseph."

Ima grew silent and closed her eyes, her lips parted in sadness as she relived the memory. I reached and took her hand, united in our experience and the hope that we clung to in the midst of our circumstances.

"You are not alone, Mary," Ima held me tight, tears rolling down the back of my neck. I wrapped my arms around her and soaked in the love of motherhood, the peace and comfort of arms.

Joseph returned with Abba as we broke our embrace. I smelled incense from the synagogue. Abba kissed Ima whose eyes were still red from tears.

"Are you well, my love?" asked Abba.

"Very well," she replied. "The Lord continues to heal.

He is good."

"Yes, indeed," Abba glanced at Joseph.

I helped Ima lay out the food, steaming. We were all hungry. We shared stories of our time with Zechariah and Elizabeth, laughing at recollections and still in awe at all that we had gone through with them. I had not realized, until today, how precious the reunion had been for Abba and Ima and I began to see the layers of redemption that were unfolding.

"We saw Savta on our walk home," Abba said.

I sat up eagerly.

"Will she come?" I asked hopefully.

"Yes, I believe she will eventually, Mary," he squeezed my hand encouragingly.

"How is she?" asked Ima.

"I don't know," Abba muttered. "She would not speak to us."

We bowed our heads as Abba began the blessing but we were interrupted by the sounds of yelling and crashing on doors throughout the village. Food tumbled to the floor as we scrambled to our feet.

"Hide!" Joseph spoke urgently. "Anah, take Mary into the grotto. Do not come out until I come for you."

"Oh, what now?" Ima cried quietly.

We hurried to the grotto and heard Abba bolt the door while Joseph secured the hatch to the roof. We sat in silence as horses hooves ripped through the narrow streets sending a wave of fear cascading through our homes.

"Open the door!" came the command from outside.

Twenty-two

We waited silently, clinging, drenched in fear. The smell of fresh bread floated into the grotto carrying with it the stench of Rome. Shouting blared momentarily and then everything was quiet. Beyond the walls of Abba's house, Nazareth lit up. Feeble questions were answered by the booming commands of the soldiers. Many times, our men had come home from encounters with the Romans beaten and torn. It was several hours before we were finally released from the grotto. The food had grown cold and the moon hung heavily in the sky.

"Come, Mary," Joseph reached into the darkness for my hand. I scrambled out and clung to him, tucking my arms in the folds of his robes, my face buried. Ima ran quickly to Abba who was panting and lying on the ground.

"I'm alright, woman," he spoke, flicking his hand in the direction of the water. "Just get me a drink."

The room was in disarray. I wondered what they were searching for, if anything. It was not uncommon for them to arrive with demands and then destroy any means we had to meet them. Abba had a gash across his shoulder, and his cheek was grazed as though he had been dragged across the ground.

"Beasts!" said Joseph, untangling me from his embrace.

He took a cloth and helped Ima tend to Abba's wounds. I salvaged what I could of the meal and we ate in silence, not daring to ask what the soldiers wanted, we were just so thankful that they had gone.

"We will sleep here," said Joseph. "It is late and I don't want Mary alone downstairs in the house tonight."

Ima and I made a pallet and I sank gratefully into it. Nazareth stirred in panic the next morning. The atmosphere was subdued and the men met early to discuss the events of the previous evening.

"Do you know what happened, Ima?" I asked while my hands kneaded dough.

"Abba and Joseph will tell us when it is time," she replied. "These burdens are for them to carry."

My imagination ran wild and I hated not knowing. I was tempted to follow them as I had when I was a child, to hide and listen. The Romans always arrived unannounced and we were never free from the tension of a potential visit. Most of the time it was to collect taxes but then they came lazily, just a handful of them. They reveled in the power of taking our money and it had been known that if they couldn't take our money, they would take our daughters to pay off debts. Many men throughout Israel had been crushed by the weight of poverty and the lack of mercy. Abba had always found a way. He and Ima were resourceful. We were poor but many other men had large families to care for. Whenever he could, Abba kept money aside to help out other families when their debt exceeded their resources. This visit wasn't about taxes though; it was fraught with energy. Our men were gone until lunchtime. Ima and I busied ourselves quietly while the women from the village passed by outside, meeting at the well where speculation ran rampant and the cries of imagined ills arose. The door finally opened and I jumped up to greet Joseph, face ashen. My chest heaved with tears.

"What is it?" I cried.

"Hush, Mary," Ima, still sitting, took my hand. "Sit and wait."

I sat reluctantly, frustrated. Joseph looked to Abba as we sat together once again to eat. The saltiness of the olives tasted so good to me. My tastes had changed with the pregnancy. I ate until the oil ran down my arms. I soaked it up with bread and waited impatiently for someone to speak.

"Rome has called for a census," Abba finally spoke. "Every man must return immediately to the place of his birth."

"A census!" cried Ima. "But it is not time."

"We cannot question Rome," Joseph interjected. "But we must be on guard."

He took my hand and shifted uneasily.

"I have been studying the prophecies. There are many indications that the time for the Messiah is imminent. Scholars and Rabbis through the ages have spent countless years studying these scriptures and there is a strong possibility that Rome is aware. Herod is an evil man. He will not take the news of a new King lightly."

"So the census is about finding the Messiah," I asked in disbelief.

"We have no way of knowing that," replied Joseph. "I am just saying that we must be cautious. We cannot predict the ways of Rome. They operate under their own law and freely abuse it at our cost. We must go to Bethlehem; we have no choice. Only God can protect the child."

"You cannot take Mary, surely," Ima spoke, eyes wide. "She is too far along to travel safely. The journey we just completed was too difficult and this one will be even further. It will not be possible for her."

"I will go," I said. "I want to be with Joseph. We will take our time and still be home in time for the birth."

I looked beseechingly at Joseph, "Please, I want to come with you."

Joseph sighed, face pressed into hands.

"Anah, if I could leave her here with you I would," he looked up, eyes tired but he spoke kindly. "You are right that this will be a difficult journey but the instructions were that family members must accompany the men. No exceptions."

Ima got up and began clearing the table. She said no more.

"We must go, Mary, we have much to do," Joseph instructed. "We leave in two weeks."

I could hardly believe that we would be traveling the same route that we had just completed, and Bethlehem would add another day to our journey. It took much preparation as Joseph had business to attend to and the weather was cooling considerably; we would need many more supplies this time. Nazareth was a bustle of activity. Some did not have to travel far so they prepared to take over the roles of those who would be gone for days, or possibly weeks. The impact on our small community was great, but we were thankful that the harvest season was drawing to a close. If this had happened even two months earlier, the impact would have been devastating.

Two weeks passed quickly and our final Shabbat was somber. The usual celebratory air was dampened by the stress of the journey ahead and the potential danger we faced. Many people would be on the road, heightening the threat from bandits and thieves. Roman surveillance would be high. The energy that I had felt earlier in the pregnancy was beginning to wane. My bones hurt, my back ached. The child lay heavily causing shooting pains down my leg and breathlessness as he pressed into my ribs. Sleeping was a chore. There was no relief whether sitting or standing. It was all taking its toll.

We left early. I shivered in the damp, cool air as Joseph hung a heavy blanket over my shoulders. The donkey shifted and I hoped that he could carry this load again for so many days. I kissed Ima and Abba goodbye.

"We will see you soon and in a few short weeks, you will be holding a grandson," I said, still holding onto Ima's hand as Joseph led the donkey away.

"Be careful," Ima sobbed, as tears poured over her fingers.

Abba put his arm around her shoulders and watched us leave, "Trust the prophecies, Anah," he whispered. "God does not make mistakes."

"What did He mean?" I asked Joseph. "What prophecies?"

He shrugged in response and I turned quickly to wave

one last time. I didn't take my eyes off them until we rounded the corner and the olive trees stood between us.

Our first few days of traveling were uneventful. The air was cool and we found many places to replenish our water supply. The greatest hardship was boredom. We had joined a small caravan at first until we had to part ways. Their company was appreciated as it wasn't wise to travel alone; their songs, and the children's play brought relief. Joseph had instructed me to speak no more than was necessary to the other women. I decided to keep to myself for fear that I might say more than I should. I was prone to trusting without question and I knew that I needed to use more caution.

On the fourth day, as daylight ebbed, we joined a large caravan that was making its way to Jerusalem. We set up our shelter on the edge of camp. It was particularly chilly and I shivered as I prepared food. Joseph tied the donkey closer to our shelter, hoping that his body heat and breath might provide us a little more warmth. So far, Joseph had sat up to keep watch while I slept, but exhaustion was setting in and I could see that he would be unable to stay awake through the night. He had spoken with the leaders of the group and felt reassured that we were in good company. I lay down and tucked the blanket around me, trying to close up any gaps where the chill could creep in. Joseph lit a small fire and lay down on the other side.

"Are you afraid, Joseph?" I whispered. Our faces were just inches apart; the fire blazed between us.

"God is with us," he replied.

His response irritated me. I knew all of the correct answers. I was raised to know, to trust, but often I didn't feel it. Darkness fell and Joseph added more fuel to the fire.

The flames lit up his face and I could see their reflection in his eyes. He looked at me, then away again.

"Yes, Mary. I am afraid. I don't know why I have been chosen to be this child's father. I am afraid that I will fail. I am afraid that I will be unable to provide for him, to protect him. I am afraid for you."

He rolled onto his back, his hands behind his head as he looked up at the sky, ablaze with stars. I kept my gaze on this man, on my husband. I had great confidence in him. It was obvious to me why he had been chosen but I knew that there was no point in trying to convince him. Only God himself could reveal whatever it was that he needed to know. I began to shiver uncontrollably as I drifted in and out of sleep. I awoke as Joseph got up to stir the fire. He picked up his blanket and came over to me. He lay down behind me and covered us both with the blanket. His arm surrounded me, his breath hot on my neck. I felt the pounding of his heart increase but he did not uncover me. I fell asleep, secure in his protection and the love of his arms.

We rose early to get a good start on the journey. Our supplies were dwindling quicker than we'd hoped; we ate only what we needed and filled our bellies with water. We said little but our eyes met and lingered, eating slowly until the camp stirred, prompting us to move on. Joseph went to the well to replenish the jugs while I rolled blankets. The dew glistened on leaves and bushes across the road where the landscape stretched; jagged hills and rocky terrain scattered with lone bushes and clusters of trees that broke up the monotony. Drops of water sat like jewels waiting to be sipped by a passing gecko or burned up by the rising sun.

Screaming from across the camp startled me and I hid behind the donkey as he whinnied and pulled on his rope.

I tried frantically to locate Joseph, not daring to leave our camp until he returned.

"Mary," Joseph called out in a breathless whisper. "Are you alright?"

I spun around, nodding my head as the jug of water he carried fell to the ground. He grabbed my shoulders and asked again, "Are you hurt?"

"No, I'm fine," I released myself from his grip and bent to retrieve the jug.

"I don't know what's happening. I didn't see any bandits or soldiers," I explained.

"Leave the donkey. We will go and find out together. We must not be separated again."

He took my hand and followed the crowd, crushing, pushing, to the scene of the uproar. As we neared we heard the shouts of men giving orders, and the long, solitary wail of a mother as she held her dying child in her arms.

Twenty-three

The group was in chaos, some closing in to assist, others dispersing in helplessness. The child had disturbed a scorpion's nest and had been stung several times. He had reacted instantly, swelling, convulsing and finally suffocating. I turned away and covered my ears as we walked back to the donkey. There was nothing that we could do. The mother's anguish was more than I could bear and I wept bitterly for her. Life was harsh; terror and death faced us at every turn. How were we to keep our child alive? Once word got out that the Messiah had been born, there would be a price on his head and on ours. I trembled.

"Are you cold?" asked Joseph.

"No," I replied.

"You must not let your faith be moved," he spoke firmly. "We cannot control what will happen. We cannot control God."

The caravan broke into two groups. We joined the one that moved ahead quickly, the rest remaining behind to bury the child and comfort the family. The events that had shaken me to the depths seemed to have made Joseph more resolute. It was as though the realization of his utter dependence on God had given him freedom.

Two more days we traveled; weariness set in. I found no position tolerable. I tried to walk but I slowed the caravan down too much. Joseph was already losing weight and I wondered if he was giving me some of his share of the food. It had taken us eight days to arrive in Jerusalem and we still had one more day to get to Bethlehem.

"Please Joseph," I begged. "Can we find a place to sleep tonight? We both need rest and a good meal."

Joseph was reluctant to stop in Jerusalem but we had missed the busyness of the Sabbath and there was a feeling of rest in the city. There were many travelers so we could easily blend in. A small inn provided a good meal, and the donkey was fed and sheltered. We slept soundly with a roof over our heads and the cold night air at bay. The threat of imminent danger eased and I dreamed only of returning home and holding my baby. We stayed to eat breakfast, feeling refreshed and clean. Men and women from all corners of Jerusalem sat together, surveying each other curiously. We ate, famished; last night's dinner absorbed by hunger and forgotten. Breakfast was devoured; steaming pots so simple but delicious.

"Your woman is hungry," said one of the other travelers

to Joseph.

"Yes, we have traveled for many days and she is expecting our first child soon," Joseph replied.

"This is not a kind journey for one in her condition." His eyes twitched as he talked and his teeth were rotten. I wanted to leave but he pressed Joseph in conversation.

"Where are you two headed?"

"Bethlehem," Joseph said. "We should be there by the end of the day."

"Wouldn't count on it," replied the man. "We're on our way back from Bethlehem. The roads are swarming with Romans and there are roadblocks all the way from there to Jerusalem. They're searching everyone. Not sure what they're looking for but I'd take the high road if I were you or it could take several days to get there."

My heart sank. Either route would be strewn with danger. We didn't know what the soldiers were looking for and didn't want to risk being repeatedly stopped and questioned; but the high road through the hills was the passageway for bandits. The man must have seen the concern in my eyes.

"We spent the last night with a group of shepherds. They travel those hills often. If you meet them, you tell them you know Dov and they'll take care of you."

I wasn't sure that I trusted this man but we didn't seem to have much choice.

"What are we going to do," I asked Joseph as we strapped replenished supplies and belongings to the donkey.

"We will follow the hills and hope that we find the shepherds," he replied.

The path was treacherous. It seemed that the higher we rose, the narrower it became. The donkey was not as sure-footed as he would have been on lower ground and he stumbled over rocks strewn before him. Joseph went ahead and kicked them out of our way but our pace was tedious. As nightfall approached I could see that he was becoming anxious. We had spent the afternoon on the down slope of the hill towards the valley and his legs were giving out beneath him. We rounded the corner and there in the valley below was a group of shepherds with a fire already lit. Their sheep huddled together and the men were cooking in a large pot over the fire. I sat up excitedly but Joseph cautioned me to be still. We made our way down the last of the slope as Joseph called out a greeting.

"We are looking for Amos, the shepherd."

"I am Amos." A man almost identical in size to Joseph stood and came towards us. "How do you know me?"

"Dov sent us. He said that we could camp with you and travel as far as Bethlehem."

Amos spat on the ground.

"Dov! Dov is a fool. Ate our food and bored us with his inane chatter. Why should I do a favor for a friend of his?" He was becoming hostile. We hadn't expected this but Joseph was resolute.

"We are going to register for the census. My wife is expecting our child in a few weeks and we have traveled from Nazareth. Please, we only met Dov in Jerusalem. You owe him nothing. I am simply asking for your company through the hills."

"Why didn't you take the road? You have made the journey difficult for her." He flicked his head at me without taking his eyes off Joseph.

"We don't have much time. The roadblocks could delay our journey by several days. Mary is strong. The highroad has added another day to our journey but we only have one more day of travel. I don't want us to be alone tonight in these hills."

"Set up your camp over there by the sheep," Amos pointed, his voice curt.

Joseph thanked him and we made our way into the valley. We lit a fire and set up the tent as quickly as we could. It was difficult to sleep. Joseph's legs ached from the climb. The sheep bleated constantly and the shepherds sang and bantered drunkenly for most of the night. We finally fell into a restless sleep before the sun rose.

"Get up!" Amos kicked at Joseph. "We leave after breakfast. You can walk with us but you will have to keep up."

Joseph leapt up and began loading the donkey.

"Get us something quick to eat, Mary," he instructed.

I found it difficult to move as pain raced down my leg. I tried to get up but dizziness forced me down again.

"What is it?" Joseph asked. "Are you sick?"

"I don't think so, I just don't think I can go on much longer, Joseph." I tried not to cry.

He helped me sit up and rubbed my back, then pulled me slowly to standing and held me while I found my balance.

"You are so strong." He brought his cheek close to mine, compassion in his voice.

"Are you two coming?" yelled Amos.

Joseph helped me onto the donkey as the dizziness passed, and quickly loaded our supplies. The shepherds were already making their way along the path with no concern for us. I handed Joseph his bread and we ate as we started out on the journey. The shepherds ignored us but we were grateful for their company. They were prepared to defend us should an animal attack and bandits left them alone, knowing that they had nothing of value to offer. We made good progress and the shepherds led us around the next hill where the path almost intersected the road. We had observed caravans of travelers from above where we were shielded by trees on the hillside. The shepherds would draw little interest from the soldiers and so we just had to wait until a quiet spot opened up. We found our opportunity as a large caravan rounded the corner. The shepherds left without a word; just a quick nod to Joseph from Amos. They would continue their journey along the beaten trail to hills that rose, twisted and gnarled around Bethlehem, dwarfing her little hill. Their stench filled my nostrils as they left, making me gag; skin oozing months of labor, dirt and the pungent smell of unbathed sheep.

The caravan was surrounded by soldiers but we blended in at the side, unnoticed. We still had several hours left of our journey but the end was close. Around the next bend we came upon our first roadblock. Blood pounded as one by one, the people before us were searched and sent on their way. Our turn came and Joseph presented our papers. I pulled my tunic tighter around my body and looked down at the ground.

"Why are there no stamps on here?" demanded the soldier.

"What stamps?" Joseph asked.

"From the other blocks, your paper should have been validated at every road block."

My heart sank and color drained from my face.

"We took the high road," Joseph explained.

"What? Why?" The soldier looked aggressive. "Do you have something to hide?"

"We wanted to get to Bethlehem quickly and had been advised that the high road would be the best way."

"Fool!" snarled the soldier. He grabbed my arm and pulled me off the donkey.

"Search them," he commanded another soldier.

I looked up with dismay and saw the face of the soldier who had attacked me in Nazareth.

"It's you!" He pointed his finger in my face and ripped my tunic open.

"So, I was right," he laughed. "Are you the father?" He pushed out his chest, intimidating, as he turned to Joseph.

"I am the father," Joseph replied, a look of confusion crossing his face.

The soldier spat at him and punched him in the stomach so that he doubled over and fell to his knees, unable to catch his breath.

"Please," I begged.

"They should have stoned you," said the soldier, spit hanging from his lips. He wiped his mouth with the back of his hand.

"They're not who we're looking for," the soldier said to his commander. "Just a nasty little wench and her *mamzer*."

"And the man?" asked the commander.

"He's a nobody." He looked over at Joseph who had recovered enough to stand up straight. The soldier smirked and pretended to launch at him again, causing him to cower. He laughed and walked away.

Our papers were stamped and we made our way through. Soldiers flanked the road. Horses snorted and shook the decorative harnesses and drapes that covered their hide. We were dwarfed by these men and hurried to join the other travelers who were equally driven to escape. The atmosphere was eerily calm as we filed past the stronghold. Not a word was spoken, but a quick glance in someone's eye revealed the fear that lurked beneath the surface. Tyranny kept us moving. The ache in my back had intensified and I was suddenly stopped short by overwhelming pressure pressing down over the baby.

"Joseph," I cried, barely above a whisper.

"Just walk," he said. "Don't look back."

"Joseph," I said again. "The baby, I think the baby is coming."

Twenty-four

"What?" hissed Joseph. "He's coming right now?"

"I don't know …. it hurts," I put my hands under my belly as the contraction passed.

"What did the midwife tell you?"

"She didn't tell me anything. We didn't think this would happen until I got back."

"What should I do?" Joseph asked. Neither of us was prepared and the soldiers were still behind, prodding us to keep moving.

We did our best to keep up with the caravan; the journey was much easier now than on the hillside. I gasped as another contraction took hold. Joseph coaxed the donkey to move quicker. We could not stop and there was nowhere to set up our tent. We wanted to be as far away from the soldiers as possible.

"It took many hours for Elizabeth to have her baby," I tried to reassure him. "I am sure we have time."

Joseph squeezed my hand and we continued. Perhaps it was the stress of the roadblock and seeing the soldiers that had caused false contractions. We stopped frequently to rest and eat; Jerusalem dominated the countryside behind us with its grand walls and towers. The Mount of Olives burst out behind, still supplying the last of its fruit. Just ahead, we could make out Bethlehem in the distance. It was a small town but the trees around it were inviting. Our pathway was largely through the desert and I was thankful that we hadn't had to contend with the summer sun. On and on we walked, the contractions didn't increase but neither did they subside. I was weak from the journey and I didn't know how either of us would survive if I had to give birth. I wondered if I would ever find relief from this relentless pressure. Peace became increasingly difficult to find anymore; just when we made plans or felt that we had some understanding of our situation, another crisis reared its head. I tracked the sun as it made its way across the sky; the colors of blue swam and changed before my eyes creating a collage of hues. Clouds danced their way above us, mocking the difficulty of our journey in contrast to their flight. As daylight drew to a close, the sun cast the brilliant glow of winter's evening across the horizon and beckoned the thunderhead of an approaching storm.

"Look, Joseph," I pointed behind as the storm drew in from Jerusalem. We could see the rain already pouring and spreading out to the right and left. Lightening flashed through the clouds. It would show us no mercy tonight. Our gentle road gave way to the rough hewn pathway leading sharply upwards to Bethlehem which clung to the rocky hillside. Massive boulders interrupted our passage, the road angling awkwardly around any terrain that could not be removed. The hills we had traveled with the shepherds were nothing compared to this. Just a few steps left me breathless and sent sharp pains firing through my body.

"I can't make it, Joseph." I clung, petrified.

Joseph's face, white, dripping, surveyed the path. His hands shook. I was losing him. I could feel it.

Travelers passed by on either side, shoving and pushing as we stood helplessly. The next contraction brought me to my knees. Suddenly, the flow of people stalled around us. Voices, then faces blurred in and out, my focus having to remain on the pain. I was hoisted onto a loaded cart. Barrels and sacks were lifted onto shoulders to make room for us. I laid back gratefully against Joseph's chest, bracing myself as the cart bumped endlessly over rocks and around curves. Joseph's voice was silent, his breath shallow.

We finally crossed through the gate into Bethlehem where we were dropped at the side of the road.

"Sorry," the cart owner spoke apologetically, helping us off, and loading his belongings back on. "Every man for himself now. I hope you can find somewhere to stay."

We were the last of the group to enter. The contractions were increasing again. I grimaced as an almighty wave surged down my belly and water gushed down my legs.

"Joseph!" I cried. "There's no time. I can't hold on!" I gripped the donkey's mane until he wailed and shook himself free.

Bethlehem bustled with energy, men spilling out of inns

and roaming the streets. Lamps burned in every window and each house was alive with noise, music and the sounds of children crying. Thunder crashed behind us as the cloud finally descended and unleashed a torrent of rain.

"We will do whatever needs to be done," Joseph tried to mask the panic in his voice.

The storm only brought more people outside, as the desert summer had been long and brutal. The cool lashings were appealing and washed away the stench of drunkeness and the grimy smell of travelers who had not bathed for days. I pulled my torn clothes in tightly, but within minutes I was soaked to the skin. I tried to catch my breath as the contractions took hold, not wanting to cry out, but it was impossible not to. The sound was quickly drowned in the beating of the storm and the carousing crowd. Joseph pounded on doors, calling out for someone to give us a room for the night. People threw objects at him from upstairs windows and yelled for him to go away.

"Can't you see we're bursting at the seams," they hollered.

We made our way down the busy street; jostled by people on every side. Their faces swam before me. Pressure bore down on my abdomen without mercy and I threw up over the side of the donkey. Shouts arose from the man closest who received the worst of the vomit and then a fight erupted. Fists flew and the glint of a knife flashed. Joseph hauled at the donkey, pulling us away. I slipped and almost fell off the blanket that dripped off the donkey's back. Shouts urged us onwards where we had almost reached the edge of town. We were out of options. We made our way down a narrow alley, the last street, small and dank. The grander inns in the center of town had lamps lit and freshly washed stone, the smell of cooking wafting into the cobbled streets. Here, the stones gave way to dirt that had muddied in the rain. We sloshed past broken doorways and rotted wood. The smells turned my stomach but still we searched. Joseph banged frantically on doors, pleading for someone, anyone to help us. Many of the homes had 'No vacancy' signs posted on their doorframes. Clearly most would only house one or two extra people besides the inhabitants anyway. I was losing hope. Another contraction, another and another.

Please, someone!" Joseph was wild with panic. "My wife is about to give birth! Can't anyone help us?" He spun, hands tearing at his hair as the rain poured in rivers over his face.

We reached the last house on the row, his fists beating the door until his hands bled.

"What do you want?" An elderly man with a long grey beard shuffled out of the house and closed the door behind him. "Can't you see that we're all full? There's no room for you here. Go away!"

"Please, my wife, she's having a baby. Do you have anywhere we can go?" Joseph asked frantically.

The man looked at me, my eyes wide with pain and fear. Pity crossed his face and he sighed, cursing the Romans for bringing such trouble to their town. He opened the door and unhooked his lantern from the inside.

"Come with me," he sighed, directing us down to the end of the alley.

Behind the house, a small enclosed field undulated with untamed earth. Large stones had settled on the left creating a makeshift wall. A barn had been constructed underneath. It was more cave than the type of stable that I was used to. The boulders wrapped around creating the back and sidewalls and then leaned overhead to make a partial roof. The front of the barn was built with wood and enclosed the front with great solid beams and sturdy double doors. We struggled across the field, torrential rain still pouring. The donkey slid in the mud and Joseph pulled me off its back and into his arms. We hurried, lightning flashing behind us, three lonely frames. The man hung the lantern inside the stable and raked the soiled hay outside, arms frail, back stooped. Joseph set me down on a small outcropping, my hair hung in strands, a pool quickly gathering at my feet. The men spread fresh hay and brought the animals to the front, leaving the driest and warmest part at the back for us. The musty smells of damp earth and manure were overpowering. I doubled over with each contraction. The pain was shocking. I turned to face the wall and leaned over as I hung on to a small ledge. The position helped to ease the pressure as my belly hung down to the ground instead of pressing down on my pelvis.

"You cannot stay here long. I am only the keeper of the field, not the owner," the man spoke fearfully.

Joseph looked dismayed.

"Just tonight," he spoke desperately. "Just leave us for tonight."

The man nodded; pity turned to compassion and he put a hand on Joseph's shoulder.

"Is there anything else you need?" he asked.

"Is there a midwife?" asked Joseph.

"Yes, but only one and there is another birth tonight. I can send word and see if she can come."

"Thank you," Joseph said sincerely. "Thank you for your help."

"It is not much, but it is all that I can offer," he replied. "May God be with you tonight."

Joseph led me to a bed of hay piled with blankets. He

peeled off my sodden clothes and attempted to dry me before helping me into a clean tunic. I lay down on my side as Elizabeth had done. The intensity of the contractions increased but I was able to sleep between each one. I was so weak that my eyes closed before the contraction had fully passed. My body shook uncontrollably. Joseph covered me with a blanket until the shaking finally subsided. The relief of sleep was overwhelming. Joseph sat back against the wall, his arms draped over bended knees, head hung low. I didn't know if he slept or prayed, maybe both for our ordeal was not yet over. The storm still raged outside but we were safe and I was thankful that we had been given a secluded place away from the wildness of the travelers. Joseph drew close and held my hand. The child that had been held in the vice like grip of the contraction squirmed and kicked as the pressure eased, his head turning and pressing my nerves; relentless pain.

The raucous sounds of town had died down, songs and foolery finally driven inside. The storm, directly overhead now, crashed thunder and lightening simultaneously. Blow after blow pounded our little shelter causing the doors to shake violently. The wind howled and screeched, unleashing fury.

I cried out, "Joseph, do something, the baby is coming."

The agony had shifted. Suddenly, I felt a powerful urge to push. Energy coursed through my body.

A lamp flashed outside. Thunder rolled and screams echoed off the boulders around us. The door opened, slamming against the wall. Rain and wind surged past the lone figure who entered quickly, stooping low into our hovel, shaking off the effects of the storm.

Twenty-five

The wind coursed through the stable, furious gusts stripped the damp walls of dripping condensation, sending sparks flying into the air and quenching flames. I grasped desperately for Joseph's hand as we were thrust into darkness. I held my breath, searching madly for a flicker of light to alleviate the panic as the walls closed in. His fingers circled mine and I felt his beard close to my cheek. The walls eased back into place as my soul clung to whispered prayers.

The child lowered down inside as another contraction took hold. I felt my face contort with pain as pressure bore down and down. I cried until my breath ran out and the groaning turned to sobbing gasps for air.

The doors swung wildly, battered against rock and walls. Rain coursed sideways, beaded jewels illuminated in blue flashes of madness. The midwife forced the doors to close and sealed them tight, then stood dripping between cow and hen, surveying our enclosure in the dimming light of lamp. Vague shadows danced eerily over beams as the whole stable hushed. I was hardly aware of anything around me, the deafening roar outside and the cacophony from the animals had become my experience, but in the sudden stillness of animals calmed, I was able to focus and I closed my eyes. I sat breathless, sweat streaming down my face while the midwife who had set a bag on the rocky outcropping peeled off soaked outer garments.

"Hurry!" Joseph urged frantically over his shoulder, my arms now around his neck as another contraction began. "We don't have long, she's ready to deliver."

The only light now was hanging at the entrance to the cave, lamp light swaying. Joseph forced words of comfort and encouragement close to my ear, his eyes wide with dismay. I leaned into his chest.

"Oh God! Help me!" I moaned, voice parched, desperate.

The midwife hadn't spoken a word to either of us, instead the hunched figure was completely focused on rekindling the extinguished fire in the corner. It took several minutes to reignite and several more to coax it back to life. A mildewed blanket was laid out beside me and a few meager supplies arranged haphazardly across it. A bowl of water steamed over the small fire that now blazed in the corner. The midwife checked me quickly and nodded, patting my knee reassuringly and then turned to gather rocks for the birthing. Joseph pulled me upright, our eyes locked. My face that had paled under the strain of labor was flushed now as I focused hard on breathing. The midwife handed Joseph a cup that he held to my lips, hands shaking; infused tea brought brief relief. I tried to work with the instincts of my body and fought the urge to resist. There was nothing left but to pass through and I wondered how anything good could come of such pain.

Joseph helped me onto the blocks and wrapped a blanket around my shoulders so that I would not get chilled but I shook it off. He moved behind me to hold me upright; I leaned my head back on his shoulder between contractions and wept. He wiped my brow and kissed my cheek. With each contraction the baby moved down, insides stretching until I thought that I might burst open.

The storm outside amplified. Wind swelled, making the roof rattle and groan overhead. Rain lashed and drove in through every open crack, howling madly. The animals whinnied and cried again, straining against ropes as the storm intensified its attack. Mice scuttled under piles of moldy hay and chickens squawked then huddled, faces buried under wings.

Weak with exhaustion, limbs sore from days of travel, soul still bruised, I called out one last time. Surely God would not abandon me now. I had no breath left, murmured prayers whispered, pathetic. Suddenly, in the midst of such intense weakness, a new power broke through. It could not come from me as I did not possess it, but it did come from within. It rose up with fury, with passion and unrelenting strength. Nothing mattered now but the deliverance of the child within. The moment had arrived and with it a substantial victory; eternal life about to be birthed. The natural world receded as I became connected with the miraculous.

Pain eased as I rose into the realm of impossibility and embraced it there. With the next contraction my tears dried. I felt the child's feet on my ribs as his back arched in his own struggle for freedom. Our lives and destinies, entwined for many months were about to collide in the chaotic and messy explosion of heaven meets earth.

With the next contraction, strength rose still. I leaned forward and grabbed the midwife's tunic, hood draped low over face. Clinging for life as the power of delivery overtook me, I pulled down until the fabric ripped open in my hands.

I collapsed into Joseph's arms to catch my breath before the final contraction came. I looked up, tunic lay open, hood shifted back. I knew those eyes. We locked, he grinned, honey breath close to mine, tattoo blazing, skin burning with holy fire.

"Push, Mary," he whispered with a grin. "Push now!"

Endnotes

All scripture quotations are taken from the NIV unless stated otherwise.

1   *Luke 1:30*
2   *Psalm 22:1 and Matthew 27:46*
3   *Deuteronomy 22:20*
4   *Luke 1:28*
5   *Luke 1:29*
6   *Luke 1:30-33*
7   *Luke 1:34*
8   *Luke 1:35*
9   *Mark 15:38*
10   *Luke 1:36-37*
11   *Luke 1:38*
12   *Excerpt taken from KEEP YOUR LOVE ON Connection, Communication and Boundaries. p.27, para. 2 Copyright © 2013 by Danny Silk. Used with permission.*
13   *Luke 1:42-43*
14   *Luke 1:44*
15   *Luke 1:45*
16   *Luke 1:46-54 The Message*
17   *Matthew 1:20*
18   *Matthew 1:21*
19   *Psalm 147:3*
20   *Luke 1:25*
21   *Song of Solomon 3:1*
22   *Song of Solomon 3:6*
23   *Song of Solomon 4:1*
24   *Luke 1:60*
25   *Luke 1:61*

26 *Luke 1:63*
27 *Luke 1:68-79 The Message*
28 *Luke 1:66*
29 *Isaiah 61:7*
30 *I Corinthians 1:27*
31 *Hebrews 12:1*
32 *Psalm 128:3*
33 *Proverbs 19:14*
34 *Song of Solomon 4:7 GOD'S WORD© Translation*
35 *Matthew 1:23 and Isaiah 7:14*
36 *Revelation 7:10*
37 *Revelation 7:12*

Glossary

Ima (Ee-ma)	Mother
Mikvah	A ritual bath for the Jewish rite of purification.
Abba	Father
Rabbi	A teacher of the Torah
Pharisee	A religious group with strict interpretation of the Law.
Bat Mitzvah	Jewish coming of age rituals for girls.
Torah	The first five books of the Hebrew bible, or Old Testament
Sabbath	A day of religious observance and abstinence from work, kept by Jews from Friday evening to Saturday evening, and by most Christians on Sunday.
Savta	Grandmother
Shabbat	The seventh day of the week and a day of rest, as commanded by God. It begins with a traditional meal and rituals.
Adonai	Lord
Tefillin	A set of small black leather boxes with verses of the Torah written in parchment and placed inside. They are worn on the forehead and the arm.

Ketubah	A document of agreement signed at the betrothal ceremony before a couple marries.
Hamuda	A term of endearment meaning, 'dear one.'
Bar Mitzvah	Jewish coming of age ritual for boys.
Betulah	A young, unmarried girl.
Mohel	A Jewish person trained to conduct a Brit Milah ceremony.
Brit Milah	A religious ceremony in which a male infant is circumcised on the eighth day of life in remembrance of the covenant between God and Abraham.
Chuppah	A canopy used in a Jewish wedding. The couple stands beneath it during the ceremony to represent their future home.
Kugel	A baked casserole, similar to a pie, made from egg noodles or potatoes.
Marriage prayer	adapted from *www.puahonline.org/jewish-prayer*
A Bride's Tefillah	Prayer before immersing in the Mikvah
Mazal Tov	Good luck
Challah	A braided loaf of bread eaten at the Shabbat meal.
Matza	Unleavened bread traditionally eaten during the Jewish Passover festival.

Mamzer   A derogatory term for a person born from adultery.

Acknowledgements

Many people have contributed their time and energy to this book through their continuous support and encouragement, reading the first proofs, recommending pertinent reading material, verifying cultural and linguistic aspects, formatting, and final editing.

My thanks go to my husband Scott and to my children, Declan, Niela and Keld who gave me the time and space to write. Also to my parents, David and Annette Herron, and to Yoav and Grace Alon, Tom Herron, Rachel Steele, Kelly Lewis, Brenda Bauer, Diana Moody, Lori Link, Moira Macdonald, Terri Blackmon, Susie Uhlik, and Philip Wilson. Finally, to Steve and Sally Wilson who will always receive my gratitude in any project that I undertake.

About the Author

Esther Hawkins, author and mother of three, moved from England to the United States at the age of twenty. Her first novel, Bedstemor, was published in 2013. This book was a gift for her family and has touched many people with a message of healing.

Esther hopes to reach out to wounded women through her books. Her passion is to share stories that break off shame and inadequacy and encourage women to take hold of the freedom and healing that is available because of the redemptive work of Christ.

Website and blog
www.estherehawkins.com
Contact me
estherehawkins@gmail.com
Facebook
Life Worth Sharing
Twitter
@EstherEHawkins

Bedstemor

By Esther E. Hawkins

A novel based on the True Life Story of Anni McCrum

From a childhood tormented by cruel sickness to an adolescence scarred by war, Anni's story of tenacity is remarkable. Traveling from Denmark to England to escape the pain of the past, she found herself facing the daily struggle of raising four children on a coal barge. For 25 years she battled through brutal English winters without running water or electricity. Anni McCrum fought to survive against the odds and has left a legacy of strength and love for her family.

ISBN: 978-1479116768

36586724R00118

Made in the USA
Charleston, SC
09 December 2014